+
Sk76m

MANWOLF

When the procession came close, Adam pulled the hood down further and covered his face with his arm. "Queen Jadwiga," he called hoarsely, "I need a miracle." Suddenly his hood was thrown back to reveal his disfigured face. Adam could see the horror in the queen's eyes as she recoiled from him and crumpled across the seat of the coach.

Adam's mother, Danusha, has always tried to hide him from the world, protecting him from the serfs' taunts about his reddish teeth, his skin ravaged by the sun. Adam doesn't know why he looks so different, but he suspects it has something to do with his father, a nobleman whom Adam has never seen and whose identity Danusha will not reveal.

Upon hearing a monk's tale that the queen can perform miracles, Adam lets himself hope that she can remove his ugliness. But when he emerges from his seclusion to beg Jadwiga's help, his deformities are exposed, and he finds himself at the mercy of a fearful mob who thinks he is half man, half wolf—a werewolf.

Adam suffers greatly as he seeks the key to his affliction and his true identity. But his suffering leads to wisdom and in the triumphant conclusion he emerges not as a victim, but as a victor.

Set in Poland in the Middle Ages, a time of great faith and fearsome superstition, this is a haunting tale of suspense and romance, of a mother and son whose destinies were both linked to the mysterious nobleman who always wore a leather mask.

MANWOLF

MANWOLF

by Gloria Skurzynski

 Houghton Mifflin/Clarion Books/New York

Houghton Mifflin/Clarion Books
52 Vanderbilt Avenue, New York, NY 10017
Copyright © 1981 by Gloria Skurzynski

Library of Congress Cataloging in Publication Data
Skurzynski, Gloria.   Manwolf.
Summary: Only when he finally reaches adolescence
does a boy, living in medieval Poland, realize people
think he is a werewolf.
[1.   Werewolves—Fiction   2.   Poland—Fiction]
I.   Title.   PZ7.S6287Man   [Fic]   80-22393   ISBN 0-395-30079-7

For Joseph Skurzynski,
his daughters, grandchildren,
and great-grandchildren,
and especially for his son.

Part One

DANUSHA

✠ ✠ ✠

Chapter 1 / *September 1382*

He waited, watching the scene below. Whether he waited patiently or not was hard to tell because of the way his face was concealed. A leather headgear covered most of his features. Scarred eyelids, half lowered, masked his eyes, which were fixed unmoving on the serfs at work in the barnyard beneath him.

One serf in particular held his attention, a tall girl who had just run laughing from the barn, her honey-blonde hair swirling around her shoulders. She deftly caught a sheaf of grain tossed to her by a man on a cart.

Still smiling, she paused, feeling the stare of the knight who waited on a small hillock twenty paces from her. As she returned his stare, her smile faded. Had she not been holding the heavy sheaf, she would have rubbed her arms to chafe away the sudden, unexpected chill which came over her at the sight of him.

Danusha had seen soldier-knights before; they often stopped at Pan Lucas's estate for a night's lodging on their travels. Never before had she seen one wearing such a peculiar face covering—the leather mask descended almost to his upper lip, and the lips were covered by a thick black mustache that curled down to his beard. No feature, no single part of his face clearly showed. Although his white cape caught the brightness of the early morning sunlight, she sensed an aura of darkness about him.

3

"Why are you standing there idle, Danusha?" the man on the cart called to her. "Why don't you carry that sheaf to the barn? This grain has to be stored before nightfall."

"Sorry, Pappa," she answered.

Her father scowled. "Have those men in the barn been bothering you? If they get too forward, call me. I'll go in there and knock a few heads for them."

"No, Pappa, they only joke with me sometimes," she replied absently. "They don't mean me any harm." With an effort, Danusha drew her eyes from the knight and went on with the work.

On the hillock, a few paces from the knight, a young squire fidgeted. He tested the straps on a pack horse and two palfreys, even though he'd checked each piece of equipment on all three horses more than once.

"Calm yourself, Marek," the knight said. "We'll wait just a while longer for Pan Lucas to appear." The squire nodded in apology, then leaned against the tallest horse and folded his arms.

Soon afterward an aging nobleman hurried up the side of the hillock, panting as he shouted, "Count Reinmar, here you are! I've been looking all over for you. I thought you'd gone."

"We stayed to thank you for your hospitality, Pan Lucas," Count Reinmar answered.

"Think nothing of it. We Polish lords are always pleased to host you Knights of the Cross," Pan Lucas lied. "We're grateful for all you do to keep the heathens away from our northern borders." That much was true.

"It's time that Marek and I started out," Count Reinmar said. "As I told you last night, we're on an important mission to Vienna. We can't delay. I imagine the High Tatra Mountains are already covered with snow." Yet Reinmar made no move to mount his horse.

The grizzled nobleman squinted at the knight, puzzled. If he's in such a hurry, then what is he waiting for, Pan Lucas

4

wondered. These Germans don't waste time talking to a Pole unless they have something in mind.

"Traveling long distances can be a hardship at this time of year," Reinmar was saying. "I have thought that this particular journey might be easier if we had a woman to cook and wash for us until we return."

So that's what he wants, Pan Lucas thought. He wants one of my servant girls, damn him. What a nuisance! Aloud, Pan Lucas said, "If you would like to take one of my house wenches along with . . ."

"A house wench wouldn't be necessary," Reinmar broke in quickly. "A field serf would be better; field serfs are used to being outside in all kinds of weather. Many nights Marek and I can't find the hospitality of a manor house like yours, Pan Lucas, or a monastery either. So we sleep in the open. That girl working with the sheaves of grain—what is she called?"

"Which one?" Pan Lucas peered down to the barnyard. "Oh, the tall one. She's Danusha, Janko's daughter. Is that the one you want?"

"She would do nicely."

"Then I'll fetch her for you." Pan Lucas strode down the hillock muttering to himself. "These German nobles—think they can ride in here and take anything they want from a Polish lord. And wouldn't you know he'd want Danusha—a big, strong girl like that, works as well as a man. Well, he'd better bring her back when he's through with her. Janko!" he called to the man on the cart. "Janko, come over here."

Janko jumped down and came to stand before Pan Lucas.

"I'm sending your daughter Danusha on a journey with that knight up there. His name is Count Reinmar von Galt, and he's on his way to Vienna on important business for the Teutonic Order. Danusha will go along to serve and cook for the knight and his squire."

"Please, master . . ." Janko bobbed his head in deference. "Wouldn't it be better to send one of the older serf women?

5

Riska, perhaps, she's a widow." Almost in a whisper, he pleaded, "Master, my Danusha is a virgin. You said she was to be married to Rydek after the harvest."

"Yes, I know I paired Rydek and Danusha," Pan Lucas answered, "but the wedding can be delayed until after she comes back—next year, even. And you don't have to worry about anything happening to her when she's with the count. He's a Knight of the Cross. He has taken holy vows."

When Janko looked doubtful, Pan Lucas stole a glance at the knight on the hillock, then lowered his voice to avoid being overheard. "God's blood, Janko! All right, I can't promise that he won't—he's a man, after all, even though he's supposed to be celibate. But I have to send her. It's politics, don't you understand? I can't offend the Teutonic Order. With the turmoil the country is in just now, we need them on our side."

"Send the widow Riska," Janko muttered. He did not look at Pan Lucas, but stood with his head lowered and his fists clenched.

"He doesn't want Riska, he wants Danusha!" Pan Lucas sighed with exaggerated patience, combing his gray beard with his fingers. "Janko, I'm a good master, am I not? If I were not, I would be having you flogged this very moment for defiance, instead of letting you argue with me. Do you think I want Danusha to go? Of course not—I'd rather keep her here. But I can't go against the Teutonic Order. And don't forget that Danusha belongs to me, just as you do. I can do anything I please with her. If I were younger I would have had her in my own bed before now, but I'm past the age for that, more's the pity. Now before I take the whip to you, as well as to Danusha and the rest of your great brood of whelps, go fetch the girl's clothes."

Janko slowly raised his eyes as color mounted to his cheekbones. "She has no clothes, master, other than the ones she's standing in."

6

"No shoes either?"

"No, master. As you say, I have many children. I cannot afford to buy cloth or leather for them until I get my share of the harvest."

"Then at least bring her a blanket," Pan Lucas said. "Surely you have some sort of blanket in your cottage. And call her over here."

When Danusha came to stand before Pan Lucas, he asked her, "Do you see that knight up there, the one in the white cape? He is Count Reinmar von Galt, a famous soldier and a man of God. He's a German; all the Teutonic Knights come from Germany. You'll travel with him to Vienna to serve him and tend to his needs."

Danusha's eyes widened. For a brief instant she felt apprehension. Not because the knight had stared at her so intently—men were always following her with their eyes—but because of the strange look of him and the feeling of ill-boding she'd sensed about him.

Noting her hesitance, Pan Lucas said, averting his eyes, "He's a Knight of the Cross—that's almost like being a priest. You don't have to worry that he'll be after you like a bull in a cow byre. He just wants you to serve him on his long journey."

Her uneasiness vanished at the last words. A long journey! For all of her sixteen years Danusha had seen nothing other than the buildings and fields of Pan Lucas's estate. Vienna, wherever it might be, would at least be different from the fields of grain needing to be harvested, the flock of little brothers and sisters who always wanted tending because her mother was too exhausted from field work to pay them much heed.

She tugged at her dress, loosening the hem, which had been tucked into her belt in front to allow her to move freely, and let the skirt fall to her ankles. She wished she had something better to wear. The dress fit her badly. It had once belonged to the widow Riska, who was not nearly so broad-shouldered or full-breasted as Danusha.

"Come along, girl," Pan Lucas said, "I'll take you to meet your new master." As they climbed the knoll, Pan Lucas added in a low tone, "Make sure you serve him properly or I'll be vexed with you. He's an important man." He pushed her ahead of him until they reached the knight.

"This is the serf you wanted, Count Reinmar," Pan Lucas announced. "You'll do me honor if you'll accept her services."

Danusha looked up at the knight, curious to examine him more closely. She was tall enough that she could ordinarily meet the eyes of any man, but Count Reinmar stood a full head taller than she did.

"Can you ride a horse?" he asked in perfect Polish.

"No, she can't, but she'll soon learn," Pan Lucas answered.

"How old are you, Danusha?"

"Sixteen, my lord."

"She's sixteen," Pan Lucas repeated, "and as you can see she's strong and healthy. No pock marks, all her teeth where they belong. I treat my serfs well."

When Count Reinmar spoke, it was as though the words came from an unknown place inside him, not from lips and tongue and throat the way other men spoke. Danusha realized it was because his mouth was so shrouded by the thick growth of hair above it. She had been staring, intrigued, as though searching for the source of his voice, but dropped her eyes so as not to seem rude.

"This young man is my squire," she heard him say. "His name is Marek."

Danusha made a brief curtsy before Marek, who appeared friendly enough. He wore a leather tunic that hung just below his hips, covering the tops of his breeches. He was fair-skinned, blond and blue-eyed, apparently a Pole because he had the coloring of so many of them, Danusha included.

8

Her father hurried up the knoll carrying a rolled-up blanket, his face set in grim lines. Grain dust clung to the stubble of his cheeks. While Pan Lucas and Count Reinmar talked together, Janko took Danusha aside to murmur, "Your mother's heart will break when she learns of this. She's working in the farthest field—there's no one I could send to bring her in time to bid you good-bye."

"Don't worry, Pappa," Danusha answered softly as she embraced him. "And tell Mother not to worry. I doubt that I'll be gone long, and I'll be serving a high nobleman. Perhaps I can learn enough so that Pan Lucas will let me work inside the manor house when I come back."

"*If* you come back," her father muttered. "We know nothing about this German nobleman. I can only pray that God will protect you."

Her father's tone made Danusha wonder whether the chance to leave the manor was as much of a boon as she'd first thought. Her arms tightened around him before she knelt to kiss his hand.

Count Reinmar seemed anxious to be on his way. "I thank you for your generosity, Pan Lucas," he said. "Marek, help the girl to mount the pack horse. It's a mare," he explained to Danusha, "and will be gentle to ride."

With Marek pushing beneath her, Danusha was lifted onto the back of the short, sturdy horse. Startled to find herself sitting so far off the ground, she clutched the horse's mane.

"Hold onto the saddlepack straps," Count Reinmar told her. "Your horse will follow mine with little urging."

Danusha's father looked stricken as the horses moved down the hillock. She wanted to wave to him but was afraid to loosen her hold on the straps; she knew she would fall. The three of them crossed the barnyard to a narrow road rutted by the wheels of farm wagons, riding through autumn-colored trees past the fields where peasants were cutting and tying grain. Danusha tried to pick out her mother among the serfs, but in the distance all the women looked alike, their heads wrapped in kerchiefs, their backs bent as they swung their scythes. None of them straightened to notice the passing riders.

They traveled in single file along the dirt road, without speaking, until they reached the last of the land which belonged to Pan Lucas. Only then did Count Reinmar turn to look at her. Danusha was swaying, her knuckles white on the saddlepack straps, and feeling a bit squeamish because of the unaccustomed motion of the horse.

Count Reinmar reined in. "Marek," he said, "dismount and let the girl ride your palfrey. Perhaps she'll find it easier if she can hold onto the pommel of your saddle. Let her keep your horse for a day or two until she gets used to riding."

After Marek had helped Danusha onto his own horse, she discovered that she felt safer in a saddle, even though the palfrey was more spirited and raised his front legs higher. She became brave enough to glance around her, at the dusty road, at the birds in the trees, and at her own bare feet in Marek's stirrups, which might have amused her had not her heart been beating so hard.

She studied the back of the knight who rode before her. His white cape, marked with a stark black cross, spread behind him and draped over the horse's heavy rump. What kind of master would he be, she wondered.

Chapter 2

Danusha was bigger and stronger than any of the other serf girls on Pan Lucas's manor. At the past harvest she'd been chosen *przodownica*, the best of the girl harvesters. While the serfs made a circle around her, solemnly watching the enactment of the age-old rite, she'd thrust a leafy birch branch into the last, choicest stalks of grain, which were always left standing. Then she reclined on a litter made of sticks and animal skins. The litter was dragged by the men around the sheaf of standing grain in a symbolic plowing of the earth. Had she not left the manor with Count Reinmar, she would doubtless have been chosen *przodownica* again for this year's harvest.

It was a pagan ceremony, performed to assure that the fields would continue to yield abundant harvests; the priest railed against the people for practicing such foolish magic. Yet, although the serfs believed fervently in God and Jesus and the Virgin Mary, they nevertheless found it wise to appease the ancient ones, the spirits of earth and sky who had inhabited the fields from the beginning of time. If they were not given their due, the spirits might make cows go dry and crops grow sparse. Or worse.

Danusha was not only strong, she was bolder than the rest. Had any of the other girls been riding through the autumn gloom of the forest where Danusha now found herself—close as it was to Pan Lucas's manor, she had never before entered

11

it—they would have been frightened by the thick growth, expecting to see forest spirits behind every tree.

The horses picked their way along a path knurled by a web of birch and wych-elm roots. Morning sunlight became ensnared above the leafy-fingered branches intertwined over their heads; the leaves glowed dully, translucent, so that they rode through a dim green and gold tunnel. Even the horses' nickering sounded muffled. If there were such things as forest spirits, if they did in fact exist, they would be held at bay by the emblem of the cross on Count Reinmar's cape, Danusha hoped. She fastened her eyes on the black cross as it moved steadily before her.

Neither her courage nor her strength could save her from the pain of riding horseback. Although used to discomfort, as all serfs were, she was not used to the feel of horseflesh between her legs or of leather rubbing beneath her. She sat stiffly in the saddle, clutching the pommel, letting the reins hang loose. Her steed followed quietly enough behind Count Reinmar's as they came out of the forest onto open ground.

After an hour she ached everywhere. Shifting from side to side, each move made her ache in a different place. The ride seemed endless, even though the sun was not yet high in the sky. When at last they stopped for the midday meal near a stream rippling through a copse of trees, and Danusha slid from the tall horse, the ground seemed to rush up to strike her strengthless legs. She wanted to crawl to the shade of the nearest tree, but forced herself to walk with as much dignity as she could command.

Sitting with her back against a tree trunk, she watched Marek open one of the saddlepacks and portion out barley bread, cheese, and apples into three equal piles. Count Reinmar carried his food some distance away and ate with his back toward them.

Marek looked at his own food and sighed. "I'm hungry as a

wolf, but before I eat I'd better take the horses to drink. Horses first, men later. That's the rule with soldiers."

Watching Marek tend to the horses, Danusha remembered that she was on this journey to serve the needs of her new master. Pan Lucas had warned her to serve him properly; she'd best ask Count Reinmar whether he wanted anything. Holding the lower branches of the tree for support, she pulled herself to her feet. Then, because each step she took hurt, she walked slowly toward Count Reinmar, her footsteps silenced by the fallen pine needles on which she trod.

When she had almost reached him, she asked, "Sir, is there anything . . .?"

He leaped to his feet and whirled on her, his eyes blazing. "Get back!" he shouted. "Never come near me when I am eating!"

Frightened, she rushed back to the tree, forgetting her soreness, and dropped to the ground as she pressed her hands against the rapid pulsing in her throat. Marek had heard the commotion and came to kneel beside her.

"I should have told you," he said. "He always has to be by himself when he eats. I don't know why—some German custom, I suppose. Don't be upset that he yelled at you. I suspect you startled him. Soldiers don't like to be crept up on from behind."

Settling himself on the ground, Marek began to eat. "Go on, eat your portion while I eat mine," he told her. "We'll have to leave in a little while."

Danusha picked up an apple but let it fall to her lap. "His gloves," she said, when she could control her voice. "He was eating with his gloves on. Is that a German custom too?"

"He never removes his gauntlets or his leather head-covering either," Marek told her. "I've been with him for a whole year, and I've never once seen his face or his hands. When he gets a chance to bathe, he makes me wait where I can't see him. They say it's because he was horribly scarred when he fought the Lithuanians."

She stared across the copse to where Count Reinmar sat, trying to imagine scars so ugly that an important nobleman would be ashamed to show his face and hands. She remembered an old beggar who used to come to Pan Lucas's manor at Christmas and stay until the snow melted. He'd been scarred in battle, too, but he didn't hide his scars, he was proud of them. He pointed them out when begging. One of his eye sockets was empty, and a rope-like scar ran from it across his face, twisting his nose grotesquely. Danusha wondered if the count could look as hideous as the old beggar had. Perhaps he looked even worse. But disfigurements were common among the peasants, and she had never been repelled by them.

"You still haven't eaten anything," Marek said, "and you'd better, because it will be hours before we stop again."

Obediently Danusha chewed and swallowed the barley bread, then asked, "Marek, are you a Pole or a German?"

"A Pole, same as you," he answered. "How else do you think I could talk to you?"

"Count Reinmar speaks our language, yet he's a German. Why is that?"

"Count Reinmar speaks many languages," Marek told her. "He's higher-born than I am, and he was educated. I wasn't. His family owns many wealthy estates in Germany, while mine owns only one small manor in Poland."

"So you're noble too?"

"I am."

"Then should I call you Pan Marek?"

He smiled. "Marek will do."

"Have you fought in battles?" she asked.

"Not yet, but I hope to before long."

"Another thing . . ." Danusha began.

"Another thing what? You do ask a lot of questions, even

14

for a woman. I'll answer one more, then you can hold your tongue for a while to let my ears rest."

"Are we going to Vienna to fight Lithuanians?"

Marek laughed. "Lithuanians don't live in Vienna, they live in Lithuania, to the north. Vienna is in Austria, to the south and west of here. Count Reinmar has to take a message to the Archduke there. And that's my last answer for now." Marek stretched on the ground and put an arm over his eyes.

Danusha would have liked to ask how far it was to Vienna, and whether Count Reinmar himself would return her to the manor when the journey was finished, but instead she ate the last of the cheese and brushed crumbs from her skirt. When she glanced up, she saw that Count Reinmar had come to stand only a few feet from her.

"I ask your pardon for speaking to you so roughly," he said quietly. "It is no fault of yours that you do not yet know my ways." He seemed about to say more but checked himself, although he continued to watch her with his dark, brooding eyes for so long that her hands fluttered to her face to feel whether she had spilled food on her chin.

After another moment he gestured toward the horses. "Time to mount."

Marek showed Danusha how to put her foot into the stirrup and swing her body onto the horse's back. When the horse began to move, all her aches flared anew, and after a short time it seemed that she had never rested at all. Count Reinmar glanced at her from time to time, but he spoke only a few words to her during the course of the afternoon.

Toward evening they came to the high walls of a Cistercian monastery. Count Reinmar rode his horse right up to the wooden gate and, still mounted, pulled on the bell rope until a white-robed monk came to greet them.

"Can you give us lodging for the night?" Reinmar asked.

"Yes and no," the monk replied. "You men can come inside with me, but women are not permitted within the monastery building. We have no place to put the woman because our guest house burned down last month. Unless she would sleep in the stable."

"She won't mind that," Count Reinmar said.

In truth, Danusha was so weary that she would have slept on the floor of the courtyard or leaning against a wall, anywhere except on the back of a horse.

Because the insides of her legs were chaffed almost raw, each step pained her as she followed Marek to the stable. She watched while he rubbed down the horses and fed them grain. After he'd cared for the animals, Marek took a pitchfork and filled one of the empty stalls with straw for Danusha.

"This should be comfortable enough," he said. "Many a time I've slept on straw myself, and many a time more I've slept with my head on my saddle and my back on bare ground."

"Thank you, Marek," Danusha said, eyeing the straw with longing. He was barely out the door when she dropped onto the pallet and wrapped her blanket around her. She slept at once.

In the morning when Marek came to saddle the horses, Danusha woke feeling better. "There's a bowl of porridge out near the well," he told her. "I left it there for you."

"Is Count Reinmar ready to leave?"

"He's at mass in the monastery chapel. He told me not to waken you any sooner than I had to."

Danusha went into the courtyard, folding her blanket as she walked. Since Marek hadn't brought a spoon, she scooped the thick barley gruel into her mouth with her fingers. It was warm and filling, having been sweetened with honey. After the bowl was empty, she licked each of her fingers, savoring the sweetness, then drew water from the well to wash her hands and face. The coldness of the water made her gasp.

She was shivering, hopping from one bare foot to the other

on the cold flagstones, when Count Reinmar came into the courtyard. Immediately she stopped her barefoot dance, but Reinmar had noticed. "Never mind, Danusha," he said. "There's a small town only a few hours' ride from here."

What does he mean, she wondered, but she didn't have time to think about it because Marek was leading the horses from the stable. Although she still felt sore, she was less afraid of riding than she had been the day before. On the road Danusha looked with interest at the fields and woods they rode through. Though they'd traveled a full day and were well into the morning of the second, nothing looked very different from the countryside around Pan Lucas's estate. Vienna will surely be different, she hoped, else I'm wearing out my hide on the back of a horse for nothing.

It was midafternoon when the walls of a town rose in the distance, its pennants fluttering above towers in the thick stone walls that surrounded it. "This must be the place he spoke of this morning," Danusha said to herself, sitting up straighter. Although Count Reinmar had said it was a small town, it looked enormous to her—its walls were a quarter mile long on each side and above the walls, steeples thrust upward into the sky. When the three of them approached the gate, a sentry came out to challenge them, but after he noticed Count Reinmar's white cape with the black cross, he waved them on.

"Where is the clothier's shop?" Count Reinmar asked the man.

"In the center of town, my lord. Turn left the next street over."

The horses' hoofs made a peculiar clopping sound. Danusha looked down, impressed and pleased to see cobblestones. Her father had told her that there were such things as paved streets; now, when she returned to the manor, she could tell everyone that she had seen them. She was gazing at the two-story houses around her—two stories, like a house

17

built atop another house—when Count Reinmar stopped in front of a narrow building with the clothmakers' guild sign outside it. He banged on the the door until it was opened.

"Is there a woman inside?" he asked the man in the doorway.

"Only my wife, my lord."

"Have her come out."

After a plump woman appeared, Count Reinmar told her, "I want to buy a warm wool dress for this girl, and a heavy cloak with a hood. Also such things as women wear beneath their dresses—clothe her from the skin out. First give her a bath. And send for shoes and stockings for her, and another blanket. Have it all done in an hour. We can't wait longer than that."

The woman looked astonished. "My lord, even with all the apprentices helping, it will take much more than an hour to make all that clothing."

"Then give her something already made."

"The only clothes already made are things which other ladies have ordered," she said.

The count took out his purse. "For an extra silver grocz, can the other ladies wait a few days for their clothes?" Though he asked it as a question, his tone showed that he expected only one answer, the answer which the woman in fact gave him.

"Yes, my lord. Certainly, my lord." The clothier's wife was all smiles as she ushered Danusha to a room in the back of the shop. "You can bathe in the wool-washing vat over there; I just changed the water," she said, pointing to a half-filled tub. "Let me take off your clothes and I'll wash you."

"I can wash myself," Danusha said, placing her hands firmly against the bodice of her dress. "I don't need anyone's help."

"Then use this crock of soft soap. Here's a rag to scrub with. By the way, why does the Knight of the Cross hide his face with a leather mask?"

"My master is a famous soldier. He was cut up in battle by the Lithuanians," Danusha answered, feeling rather proud to convey such news. "His face is so scarred that he covers it so people won't be frightened."

"Does it frighten you?" the woman asked.

"I haven't seen his face, but I know that if I saw it, I wouldn't be afraid."

The soap was harsh and smelled of fat, but the hot water soothed her sore muscles. After Danusha had scrubbed her body, taking care not to let the strong soap touch her chafed thighs, she washed her hair, then dried it with some rough linen the woman had left near the vat.

"Is there a comb I can use?" she asked, climbing out of the tub, trying to cover herself with the linen.

"I'll get my own—it's behind the shop." The woman returned with the comb and stood watching Danusha untangle the snarls from her long hair. "Why don't you keep the comb, miss?" she asked impulsively. "My own hair is so thin now . . ." Then her face clouded as though she regretted the offer.

Half an hour later Danusha smoothed the rich wool she wore. She hadn't known that dresses could be made to look so fine; dark green, this one was, cut with a round neck and long sleeves. The gray cloak had a lining of rabbit fur and was trimmed with squirrel.

She worried as she reached to pick up the shoes. Her feet were so big—if the shoes had been made to fit some fine lady, they would surely be too small. But evidently there were fine ladies with big feet, too, because the shoes went on nicely.

Feeling shy, because never in her life had she hoped to be so richly dressed, she presented herself to Count Reinmar.

His eyes traveled over every part of her, from her clean, shining hair to her new shoes, but he did not comment on what she wore. Instead, he said, "Hurry and mount. We've been here longer than an hour."

19

Danusha had trouble arranging the thick skirts over the horse's back—how did noblewomen manage, she wondered. Then she forgot about the skirts because there was so much to see. She wished she could ask Count Reinmar to go more slowly. The town's narrow shops flanked each other, each with a sign over the door picturing the merchandise sold inside—shoes, animal skins, pots of tin and of copper. The stone church in the middle of the square was so tall that she leaned backward in the saddle to see the top of it. From its doors came the sound of choirboys singing and the scent of incense. Stalls of vendors lined the square, displaying pumpkins, cabbages, onions and other fruits of the harvest; the vendors hawked their wares in loud voices. Before she could begin to sort out the strange sights, sounds, and smells of the town, they'd reached the outer wall.

To make up for the hour they'd lost in town, they traveled longer that day. Only a faint duskiness remained in the sky when Count Reinmar raised his hand for them to stop, somewhere in the middle of a woods.

"We will have to spend the night here," he said. "The next manor is too far, and there are no inns on this part of the road."

After Marek built a fire, Danusha skinned and roasted a hare which he'd bought in the town, taking pains to see that not a drop of blood or grease fell on her new dress. She was not so good at cooking—the hare was burned on the outside—but both men ate it without complaint.

Count Reinmar sat in shadow, out of reach of the firelight, as he chewed on a blackened leg of hare. Danusha was careful not to go near him or even look his way as he ate. After he had finished he called out, "You can sleep first, Marek. I'll wake you when it's your time to watch."

"Thank you, sir." Marek yawned and stretched, put a few more sticks into the fire, then wrapped a blanket around him as he curled up near the heat.

20

After she'd eaten her own meal, Danusha made herself a bed of fallen leaves. She placed her old blanket on top of them. Lying down, she covered herself with the new blanket and her gray cloak, feeling warmer than she ever had at that time of year. As she turned on her side, the leaves crackled beneath her, releasing a pleasant autumn aroma which for some reason reminded her of home.

She wondered whether her younger brothers and sisters were missing her. Yet she had no regrets that she'd been chosen for this journey. When she returned home, she could tell the children about the things she'd seen, and about Count Reinmar's kindness in buying her clothes intended for a woman of high birth. She stroked the fine wool of her dress, savoring its softness as her eyelids grew heavy.

She was almost asleep when she felt a gloved hand cover her mouth. "Don't cry out," he whispered.

Chapter 3

Danusha was silent and heavy-hearted in the morning as they prepared to leave. She'd remembered as soon as she opened her eyes that she was not the same. A disgraceful thing had happened to her the night before—that violation of the body, that deflowering which the unmarried girls feared and whispered and giggled about at home on the manor.

She glanced at Count Reinmar through lowered eyelids, wondering whether he'd act any different today than yesterday, but he seemed unchanged. He helped Marek to load the pack horse, then adjusted his own palfrey's harness, whistling under his breath. It was always this way, the older women had told her, wagging their fingers and pursing their lips angrily. Men do this ignoble thing to girls, then walk away as though nothing has occurred, while the girls worry and suffer and wonder whether anyone will find out.

Tears stung her eyelids as she thought about her parents. Her father had looked so distressed when Danusha went away that surely he'd suspected this was going to happen. Then why had he let her go? No, she couldn't blame her father. He belonged to Pan Lucas the same as she did; their whole family was Pan Lucas's chattel. Her father had always been so careful of her, trying to protect her from the rough jokes and oglings of the men on the estate. How it must have hurt him to see her leave!

She thought fleetingly of Rydek, the serf who was her betrothed. They were to have been married in a few weeks, but now. . . . Rydek mattered least of all to her. The marriage had been arranged, Rydek chosen for her by Pan Lucas. He was not a bit different from any of a dozen other young serfs on the manor, no better, no stronger, a bit more handsome perhaps, but certainly no more clever. She shrugged, dismissing him from her thoughts.

Climbing onto the saddle of Marek's horse, Danusha blushed as she swung her leg over the horse's back. It hadn't occurred to her before, but she must look like a wanton sitting astride that way, with her legs spread apart. Her face grew hot with shame.

"But what could I have done to stop him?" she asked herself. Count Reinmar was a nobleman; noblemen were entitled to take what they wanted. He had treated her well enough, asking her pardon the one time he'd shouted at her. Pan Lucas would never have apologized to a serf. He'd dressed her like a lady, and told her to ride Marek's horse even today, when she knew she could have managed the pack horse.

God has set the nobles over us, she reminded herself, and we have no choice except to obey them. If they treat us badly, we must bear it and not complain, because after we die and go to heaven it will all be made up to us. Then she shuddered. Could it be possible that she wouldn't go to heaven after she died, now that she had lost her virginity?

"Holy Blessed Virgin, it wasn't my fault!" she said half-aloud. "Sweet Jesus, you know it wasn't my fault. Surely I won't be sent to Hell for something I couldn't help!"

Count Reinmar's palfrey broke into a gallop and Danusha's horse followed, whinnying as it picked up speed. She drew on the reins to slow him, but then she loosened the reins and let him run.

Her hair streamed behind her as she half-rose in the stirrups, realizing that she had picked up the horse's rhythm and could ride without fear. It felt good to ride in the wind, good to be a part of the world outside Pan Lucas's estate.

And if she had to lose her virginity, she reasoned, wasn't it better to have lost it to a nobleman who had been decent to her otherwise, rather than to some drunken lout of a serf who might have pulled her down behind the bushes? That happened often enough at the manor.

Her horse caught up to Count Reinmar's and they galloped side by side. Then Reinmar gave his steed full rein, racing faster and faster, but Danusha stayed beside him. Hoofs pounded dirt; she felt merged in the powerful unity of horse and rider as they flew down the lane with her palfrey's neck stretched forward like a lance. Even if she could not control her destiny, for at least a few exhilarating moments she was in control of her body and the hurtling beast beneath her. It was Reinmar who finally pulled back.

Breathless after the hard ride, Danusha caught herself smiling.

The next night they slept in the forest, the following night at an inn. Both nights Count Reinmar lay beside her. Marek must have known what was going on between them, but he didn't seem concerned. Marek worshiped his knight and thought all his actions were godlike.

And over the next few days, Danusha herself began to admire the count—his deep voice, his air of authority, his knowledge of the countryside. Once she heard him softly singing a Polish peasants' tune, "Fly not here, bright-winged falcon . . . no more shall we come to this field. . . ."

A phrase they used on the manor came to her mind: *hart ducha,* a quality of spirit which did not permit fear in oneself, or compromise, or defeat. Reinmar had *hart ducha.*

He was not as old as she'd first thought. It had been hard to judge his age because she never saw his face or hands, but from his vigor and body stance she guessed, as she watched

24

him almost constantly out of the corners of her eyes, that he was in his early thirties. The concealment of his face began to seem less strange to her, a natural part of him.

When he came to her at night, Danusha sensed that he tried to treat her gently, and sensed also that he might be as inexperienced in these things as she was, but of that she was not certain, knowing little enough about the ways of men and women together. And when he wanted her to perform a task, he spoke not as a master to a serf, but as she imagined noblemen spoke to their ladies. "If you please, Danusha . . ." he would say.

At the end of the first week Danusha was in love with Reinmar.

Chapter 4

The blizzard raged around them like an eruption from Hell, hurling stinging ice crystals into Danusha's eyes. She'd wrapped the blanket around her head, allowing just enough of an opening so that she could see, but there was nothing to see except white violence. She prayed to God that Reinmar was still riding ahead of her and Marek behind. If she lost her way in this fury of wind and ice, they would never find her.

Three weeks earlier she'd been a serf girl sweating under the harvest sun; now she was a knight's woman, freezing with him on a treacherous pass in the High Tatra Mountains.

She leaned against the pack horse's neck, attempting to shield herself from the storm while she drew warmth from the straining beast. Reinmar and Marek were riding the stronger palfreys, one leading Danusha and the other following to protect her from the wild weather.

When the pack horse lurched, Danusha was thrown forward. She tried to wrap her arms around its neck, but the animal floundered, dropping her into the snow. "Reinmar!" she screamed. Over the howling of the wind he couldn't hear her, but Marek reached her and scrambled off his horse to help her up.

"Are you hurt?" he asked, as he brushed snow from her cloak.

"I'm all right. The horse pitched forward. I don't know why."

The pack horse whinnied, rolling its shoulder in the snow as it tried to rise to its feet. "Looks like it's gone lame," Marek shouted. "God, what a place for this to happen! I'll ride ahead to get Count Reinmar."

Danusha waited, feeling shut off from the world as the whiteness swirled around her, the wind shrilling like evil spirits bent on tearing flesh from her bones. She had never felt so alone. The world had disappeared from sight except for the crippled horse, which was now standing beside her. Her feet grew so numb that she thought they would break off if she moved them.

Then Reinmar appeared like an illusion through the whiteness, with Marek following him. He said nothing as he knelt to examine the pack horse, raising its leg and running a hand over its shank and hoof.

"The leg isn't broken, thank God." He bellowed to be heard over the wind. "Lead it into the trees for shelter, Marek. Bring all the horses together for warmth while I decide what to do."

Danusha huddled between the animals as Reinmar and Marek talked with their heads close together to be heard above the noise of the storm. Most of their words were blown away, so that Danusha couldn't understand them.

She worried over this new delay. They'd been held up for ten days in Nowy Targ while Reinmar waited for the arrival of another knight who was to bring the Great Seal of the Teutonic Order. Without the imprint of the seal, Reinmar had told her, any papers he signed in Vienna would be valueless.

If they hadn't been detained for so long in Nowy Targ, they could have passed this crest of the Tatra Mountains before the storm came. Now, with the pack horse gone lame, they would be delayed even more.

One moment the storm was blowing with ungodly fury, the next moment the wind died to a moan. Snow began to fall with enough distance between the flakes that the world emerged once more. The blizzard had not brought deep snow; patches of earth and rock were blown clean with only a thin coating of ice on them. The gray sky changed to the color of pearl and then brightened, showing that it was still only late afternoon.

"Find some branches to start a fire, Marek," Reinmar said. "We'll spend the night here." Reinmar unstrapped the saddlepacks from the lame horse, which stood with its legs apart and its head lowered to the ground. "I'll build a shelter under that large pine against the rock."

"Will the pack horse be able to travel again, Reinmar?" Danusha asked him.

"I doubt it. See how its shank has begun to swell? This mountain pass is difficult to maneuver even with good horses. The storm seems to have passed—these autumn storms don't last long—but another one might blow up before we're over the crest of the range."

"Count Reinmar!" Marek was hurrying toward them, his arms full of broken branches. "There are men ahead on the pass. I couldn't believe my eyes when I saw them here in this desolate place."

"Who are they?"

"A band of five—five monks from the Cistercian abbey near Krol Forest, the one where we stayed the first night Danusha was with us. They're returning from a conclave in Prague, they told me. They're just ahead, traveling toward us on foot."

"Ride back, Marek. Ask them to join us for the night. Find out which one of them is in charge, and say that we'll share our food with them. Tell them anything, only make sure to bring them back here."

28

As they waited for Marek to return, Reinmar hunched on the ground, attempting to make the pack horse put weight on its lame leg. Danusha unwrapped the blanket she'd worn around her head; since the wind had died, it was not so cold. For a brief moment the sun broke through the clouds, turning trees and rocks into a blaze of bright ice crystals. Danusha would have enjoyed the beauty of it had Reinmar not been so concerned about the horse.

They heard the crackle of brush as Marek came into view, riding slowly to lead five white-robed monks toward them. Reinmar got to his feet and went to meet the men.

"God be with you, Brothers," he said. "This is a strange place for men of God to meet. I am Reinmar von Galt of the Teutonic Order."

"May the rest of your journey be more comfortable than this past hour has been, my lord," a round-faced monk answered, shivering. "The storm made me thankful that I'm not one of the barefoot friars. I am Brother Vincenty." He raised his hand in the sign of peace. "Your squire tells me that you're bound for Vienna."

"And already too far behind on our journey," Reinmar said. "I'm going to build a shelter for the woman while the daylight lasts. After that, and when we've eaten, I would like some talk with you, Brother Vincenty."

The monk nodded, eyeing Danusha with interest.

For the next hour Reinmar cut branches to build a lean-to at the base of a large pine while the rest of the men used branches to sweep a clearing around the fire Marek had started. Their talk was sporadic as the group settled around the fire to eat bread and dried meat. Reinmar carried his food away from the men, saying that he'd examine the lame horse again as he was eating.

The lean-to was far enough away from the fire that Danusha didn't hear what the men discussed while she made

29

up her bed under the tree. By the light of the campfire she could see Reinmar and Brother Vincenty talking quietly. The other men lay curled on the ground, their cloaks wrapped tightly around them even though they were as close to the fire as they could get. She wondered whether Reinmar would come to her with so many people nearby, and she tried to stay awake to wait for him, but she was weary after the violence of the storm. The pine needles felt soft under her. She slept.

In the middle of the night she awakened to his touch. The sky had cleared; through the branches of the lean-to she could see stars more luminous than the ice crystals had been with the sun on them.

"I have to talk to you," Reinmar whispered, "but we must speak quietly so the monks don't hear us."

She reached to take his head between her hands. "Lie down and let me warm you."

He wrapped his cloak around her, and they pressed together; she savored the closeness of his body. "Danusha," he murmured, "I have to say certain things to you tonight because . . . Danusha, I curse myself for what I've done to you."

"Don't, Reinmar." She touched his mouth with her fingers. "For what has happened between us, you can't blame yourself unless you blame me too. I've lain with you willingly enough these weeks past."

He was silent for a long time, then he whispered, "There are things about me that I want you to understand. I was sent to the Order when I was very young, younger than Marek. Your age. I took the vow of celibacy, and mostly I've kept it. But I'm not like other men. I wish to God that I were, but . . . I'm horrible to look at."

She would have stopped him, but he shook his head. "No, listen to me. You've never seen my face. If you had, you would not be so kind to me."

"The way you look could never matter to me, Reinmar. I'd love you if . . . ."

30

"Let me go on. I know what I am and for the most part I've accepted it. Sometimes, though, when I see how other men live, terrible moods come over me. In the time before I came to Pan Lucas's manor, I'd drowned myself in pity for a long while, wishing I could have the comfort of a woman. Then I saw you, and I decided to take you. I did you a terrible wrong."

"Reinmar, stop!"

"Danusha, it would take more courage than I have to let you see my face, but here, feel my hand. I've taken off the glove. Do you feel the scars? Put your hand on mine."

She traced her fingertips over the back of his hand, feeling welts raised so close together that the hand seemed covered with continuous scar tissue. The nails were ridged, and on one finger there was no nail at all.

"I can't even straighten them," Reinmar told her. "The scarring has drawn my skin so tight that my fingers are always curved. My face is even worse."

"It doesn't matter in the least to me," she assured him. "I love you because you're strong and decent. No living man could be better than you, Reinmar. Take off your mask and I'll kiss your face to show you that . . ."

"Don't ask me to do that, Danusha. I cannot. I'm only telling you these things because I want you to know that . . . that I don't make it a practice to carry off women for the sake of lust. I've never done it before, and I wish to God that I hadn't hurt you this way. I was wrong to take you from the manor. I want you to forgive me."

"There's nothing to forgive, Reinmar."

He sighed and turned away from her. "Danusha, I have to send you back."

"Send me . . ." She raised herself from the ground, trying to see him in the dark.

"I have no choice. The pack horse is lame—it can't carry weight. The monks will lead it down the mountain."

31

"Reinmar, I'll walk behind you. Don't send me back! I want to go with you!"

"Hush, Danusha. They'll hear us. If I try to keep you with me, it will only make things worse. I have a duty to the Order, and you—you're young enough that you can forget me."

"Do you think I give my love so lightly?" she asked, choking on the coldness that settled inside her breast.

"Brother Vincenty will take you as far as the monastery," Reinmar said. "From there you'll find your way back to the manor—you can walk the distance in two days. Danusha, I don't want to do this, but there's no other way. You may feel pain now, but you're not much more than a child. In time you'll find another man to love."

Danusha felt ravaged with hurt and disbelief, but she would not let herself plead with him. "So you intend to cast me off," she said, unable to keep the bitterness from her voice.

"I wronged you," he answered. "If I kept you longer, it would make a worse wrong. But cast you off? No. I'll give you money so that you can buy what you need to live decently."

"Money! Men give money to their whores."

He grasped her shoulders so tightly that she sucked in her breath. Although he spoke quietly, she could feel his vehemence. "Can't you bring yourself to believe me?" he asked. "What I'm doing is best for you. There's no way we can have a life together. If you stayed with me, you would suffer far more than you're suffering now. I value you too highly to let that happen. And I cannot throw away my commitment to the Order."

"God damn the Order!" Danusha whispered hoarsely.

"God has already damned me," Reinmar muttered. "Take the money, Danusha. Don't be foolish. Keep it for a time when you may need it." He groped for her hands and pressed coins into them, saying, "It will be light soon, and we'll have

32

to leave each other. You must feel hatred for me now, but I
. . . regret—believe me that I deeply regret—Danusha, I have
come to love you."

At last she allowed herself to cry. She fell against him and
sobbed, feeling his arms around her for the last time.

Chapter 5 / *June 1383*

Danusha wiped the perspiration from her face and moved her heavy body to the side of the hearth to escape the heat. Another pain started in her back and worked around to the base of her swollen belly; the pains had begun at midday. "Holy Virgin, not now," she prayed. "Not here." She looked around at the smoke-stained walls, the matted rushes on the floor. If only she could hold off until she finished preparing the evening meal for Pan Lucas, then she could go into the woods and have the baby where the air was clean, not fetid with the smell of onions and grease. She held her body rigid, waiting for the pain to spend itself.

"Danusha, are your pains becoming hard?" the old crone Kasia asked her. Kasia had been sitting on a stool, resting her feet.

"They are," Danusha admitted.

"Do you want me to fetch your mother?"

"No!" If her mother came, wearing the look of hurt she'd worn since Danusha's condition had become apparent, the birthing would be twice as hard. "Don't call her, Kasia. I don't want her to come until after it's over."

"Very well, then. You'd best go lie down. I'll finish turning the meat," Kasia offered.

"I'm not going to give birth here, Kasia, not in this place. I'll go outside somewhere." Danusha panted as another pain started.

"It's too late for that, my girl, if you'll take my advice—and you'd better, because I know all about these things," Kasia stated. "Besides, you're better off here where I can help you. Don't worry about anything. These old hands of mine have caught many a baby as it fought its way into the world. I've been *babka* to a whole horde of them."

Danusha looked at Kasia's hands, at the black lines of dirt embedded in the seams, the ragged fingernails. "At least wash your hands before you attend me, Kasia."

"What for? Oh, very well. Such a lot of fuss about nothing," the old woman scolded. "You do have foolish ideas since you came back from that nobleman." Kasia plunged her hands into a tub of water warming on the hearth, made a few scrubbing motions, then shook drops of water onto the floor. "There, is that better? There's clean straw in the corner—go lie on it and scream your head off if you want to. I've always believed that screaming helps with birthing , especially when the child has no father."

Danusha spread a square of linen on the straw—she'd saved it for this time—then took off her dress to lie down. Her pains were coming closer together.

"Now, I can go on turning the meat while I keep an eye on you," Kasia said. "Don't worry, I'll be beside you when you need me. You shouldn't have any trouble, a broad-hipped girl like you. Having a baby is nothing unless the cord gets wrapped around its neck, or if it comes sideways. If this one doesn't come fast enough, I'll reach up to give it a little pull."

Danusha shuddered, wishing she'd been able to leave the kitchen house. Old Kasia meant well, and she was wise enough in everyday matters, but she was slovenly and bent with the aches of old age. After Danusha had returned to the manor and had been assigned to help Kasia in the kitchen house, she'd attempted to keep the place cleaner. But Kasia had let her know from the first that things were to be done

35

exactly the way Kasia wanted them done, the way they'd always been done.

Danusha noticed Kasia stuffing rags into the crack beneath the kitchen-house door. "What are you doing?" she asked.

"Sealing all the chinks to keep out any evil spirits who might harm the little one when it comes," the old woman replied. "I wish I could seal the smoke vent, too, but to do that I'd have to put out the fire. Then the meat wouldn't get cooked, and Pan Lucas would yell his head off. Well, as long as the smoke keeps drifting upward, that means no evil spirit is trying to come down through the smoke hole." She cast a wary eye on the blackened opening in the ceiling.

After a while Danusha felt warm wetness gush from her body. When Kasia came to have a look, she said, "Not much longer now, my girl. Why don't you yell a bit? It helps, it truly does." She pushed gently on Danusha's belly.

A scream escaped her as Danusha bore down hard, then hard again. After what seemed an endless time, although it was only midevening, the baby came forth. For a moment Danusha lay panting, realizing that it was over, then she bent to look at the bloody little mass that had been inside her. The fire in the hearth gave enough light that she could see him clearly when Kasia picked him up, holding him head down to clear the birth matter from his mouth.

"A nice, healthy little boy," Kasia said, as the baby began to cry in a long, loud wail. "Let me cut the cord, then I'll clean him. You didn't have such a hard time, now did you? That was fast for a first one."

When Kasia laid him in her arms, Danusha wanted to weep. He was beautiful, a perfect baby who would never know his father. He looked nothing at all like her younger brothers and sisters; she remembered them as infants, blond and blue-eyed. This baby had thick black hair and eyes which promised to be dark. He must look like Reinmar, but how would she ever know?

The first time Danusha changed his linens, she cried out in surprise. They were stained pink. "Kasia, come here, look at this," she called. "Look at the wet stains on this cloth!"

"Well, gracious God, I've never seen anything like that before!" Kasia exclaimed. "Maybe it's something that will pass. He seems healthy enough—he sucks well, and he squalls good and loud. But I've never known a child to wet his breechcloth pink like that."

Danusha's face twisted with alarm. "Do you think there's something wrong with him?"

"No, no, he's a fine baby. I haven't seen a better one, and I've seen a lot. If his urine is a bit strange in color, what does it matter? Maybe it will go away when the priest baptizes him. What are you going to call him?" Kasia asked, trying to turn Danusha's attention from the pink-stained cloth.

"Tell me the truth, Kasia. Are you sure it's nothing serious?"

"Of course not, girl. I've been around enough newborns to know when one's sickly. This one isn't. And I've seen stranger things than that with new babies. Did I ever tell you about the time I delivered one that already had a tooth? When his mother put him to nurse, he bit her on the breast. Oh, did she ever holler! Nearly threw him across the floor." Kasia cackled, at the same time looking sharply at Danusha to see whether the story had distracted her. "You didn't answer me. What will you name your son?"

"Adam. Months ago I decided on that name." Danusha was examining the baby carefully, running her hands over his body. "He seems fine otherwise, Kasia. Do you think . . ."

"Adam." Kasia grinned, showing her few yellow teeth. "The first man—at least the first one ever born in Pan Lucas's kitchen. It's a good name for a strong man-child. You rest now, Danusha. I can do the kitchen work for the next few days."

By the second day after Adam's birth Danusha noticed that Kasia's face looked gray and her breath was coming short. Although she claimed not to know her age, Kasia was a very old woman, already bent when she'd come to work as Pan Lucas's cook. Danusha got up to put on her dress, tucking her long hair up under the cap she wore now that it was no longer seemly for her to wear her hair loose like an unmarried girl. She went to Kasia and lifted the iron cauldron from her hands.

"Thanks, dearie." Kasia smiled weakly. "Are you sure you're fit enough to start working?"

Danusha nodded. She felt strong, and Adam was a good baby who did not demand much attention. As the weeks went on and Adam grew normally, she worried less about the pink color of his urine which stayed the same, even after baptism.

Although the work in the kitchen was hard, it allowed Danusha time to care for her child. By the end of autumn when the last of the harvest had been stored and the ground grew hard with frost, Adam could sit up and wave a wooden spoon to amuse himself. If Danusha was too busy to tend him, Kasia went to Adam—the old woman doted on the child.

On a day near Christmas Kasia sat bouncing Adam on her knee to make him laugh. Danusha hummed softly as she rolled a pastry crust on the table, but when she glanced up from her work to smile at her son, she noticed that Kasia's face had clouded.

"What's the matter, Kasia? Do you feel sick?" she asked. "Do you want me to take Adam?"

"No. No." Kasia frowned, sucking in her lips so that her nose almost touched her chin. "Adam has a tooth."

"He has? Oh, let me see. His first tooth." Danusha wiped

her hands on her dress, then knelt next to the baby and gently opened his lips. "Where is it? There it is!" Her face contorted. "Kasia, look at the color of it! His tooth is pink!"

Kasia licked her lips. "Well, the pink urine hasn't seemed to hurt him, and a pink tooth should bother him even less, wouldn't you say, Danusha? Here, girl, why are you crying? It's nothing to get upset about."

"Oh, Kasia, no one will see him when he makes water, but everyone will see his teeth! What's wrong with my baby?"

"Ah . . . who ever gets to see him anyhow?" Kasia grumbled, stroking Danusha's hair. "Both of you are shut up in this kitchen every day of your lives—Adam will grow up thinking the whole world smells of onions! The serving girls never pay him any attention, and Pan Lucas hasn't been in the kitchen since I got here, however many years ago that was. So who will notice? Now quit your carrying-on. He's a fine baby, the smartest I've ever seen. Look at him pulling your hair. He wants to comfort his mother."

Danusha sank to the floor, distraught. She had never heard tell of such unnatural traits as marked her baby. No one in her own family showed any such signs . . . could they be oddities which came from his father? She realized that she had never seen Reinmar's teeth. His mustache covered his mouth—was *that* why he always went off by himself to eat? His teeth were discolored like Adam's!

She turned in horror to stare at Adam. *The scars!* "I am not like other men," Reinmar had told her. "I wish to God that I were." Had Reinmar really been cut in battle, or was the scarring another affliction of some terrible malady he had passed on to his son?

She tore Adam's shirt to search his skin for any kind of mark, startling Kasia who cried, "Here, what are you doing? You nearly pulled him off my lap!" Adam's skin was flawless, as Danusha's mind had already told her it was. Fear alone made her scrutinize every fold, every surface of his smooth body. She picked up his hands. Reinmar had said that he couldn't straighten his hands; Adam's were soft and pliable. She pressed them flat against her palm. Adam pulled away, looking solemnly at her with his large dark eyes.

Danusha grasped her baby and held him tightly against her breast. If only God would keep any further affliction from Adam, she could manage. She would keep him away from people as much as possible. Her son was not going to become an object of ridicule, even if she had to spend her whole life fighting to protect him.

Chapter 6 / *October 1384*

At sixteen months, Adam ran around the kitchen and talked in sentences. Danusha knew that he was an extraordinary child and would have liked to show him off to all the women on the manor, but she kept him secluded because of his teeth. All his teeth had come in with colors ranging from pink to a deep, dull red.

Danusha's hours were filled with work because Kasia's joint aches had grown so much worse that she could no longer move about without pain. The old woman sat on the doorstep of the kitchen house to enjoy the sun, gossiping with anyone who passed. Adam wanted to go outside with Kasia, but Danusha wouldn't permit it.

Once when Kasia had left the door slightly ajar, Adam slipped out and ran to the well in the courtyard. Danusha rushed to catch him, slapping his bottom again and again until Adam screamed and Kasia seized Danusha's arm, shouting, "Stop it! You're hitting him too hard!"

"Let me alone!" Danusha cried, pulling her arm free. "I have to teach him that he can't come out here. I know what's best for him."

"Best for him! You're acting like a crazy woman, bruising his backside like that. What's worse, you keep the poor little thing in a prison."

Cheeks flaming, Danusha turned on Kasia. "He's my child, not yours!" she shouted. "I'm the one who must keep him from being laughed at." Then she began to cry. "Oh, Kasia, I'm sorry. You're so good to both of us . . . I don't know why I . . ."

"There, there. Pick up the little fellow and comfort him, dearie. No wonder you get all worked up. It's not only Adam who's a prisoner; you are too, with nobody to talk to day in and day out but an old wretch like me." Kasia put her arm around Danusha's waist and coaxed her along. "Come inside now, and we'll soothe ourselves with a sip of mead. I know where Pan Lucas keeps the best of it. Little Adam can have a drop too. He'll sleep better for it."

The quarrel had ended as quickly as it began, but from then on Danusha saw to it that the door was firmly shut each time Kasia went out to sit on the doorstep.

It was a day in the beginning of October when Kasia shuffled inside, her eyes glittering with excitement. "Danusha, wait till I tell you what I've just heard! There'll be a tizzy around here the likes of which you've never seen. Get me a chair, dearie, and help me into it so I can tell you the news."

"Heavens, Kasia, hurry up and tell me," Danusha said, running with a stool to place it beneath the old woman.

"Well!" Kasia grinned with the importance of her announcement. "We're to have a new queen, after fourteen years without anyone on the throne—you already know that. But listen to this! Even now, Queen Jadwiga is on her way to Poland. The day after tomorrow, she's to pass right by here on her way to Krakow. Pan Lucas has said that everyone from the manor may walk to the road and cheer as the young queen goes past."

"Everyone?"

"Yes, everyone who can walk the four miles to the road." Kasia's expression saddened. "Of course, I couldn't possibly do that, but you can go, Danusha. You go and notice every-thing, then come back and tell me all about it."

"Maybe you could go too, Kasia," Danusha said. "Some of the men could carry you in a chair."

"Four miles over and four miles back? Don't be foolish, my girl. No one would want to haul this old bag of bones that far."

"A cart!" Danusha said. "I'm sure Pan Lucas would let you ride in a horse-drawn cart."

"The path through the forest is too narrow for a cart, I've already inquired about that," Kasia told her. "But as long as you're there, and see what there is to see and tell it all to me, I'll be content. I'll stay here with Adam. You won't want him to go, because all the people would see . . . you know."

Danusha had to agree that it would be best for Adam to stay with Kasia. "Who told you all this?" she asked.

"Riska. She was just on her way back from cleaning Pan Lucas's best clothes—he does have a habit of spilling wine on his tunics. He's to join the procession as it passes, then he'll go the rest of the way to Krakow for the coronation. That's why he wants our people along the road, I suppose, to show his support for the new queen, after all the delays we've had in getting her here from Hungary. Fourteen years without anyone on the throne, and now we have Jadwiga! Blessed be her name."

"I've heard that she's a beauty," Danusha said. "Oh, of course, it was you who told me that. You heard it from Riska."

"Who heard it from Pan Lucas, who heard it from a member of the Sejm Parliament who stayed here a month ago. Jadwiga's mother tried to keep her from coming here to be our queen—I think she believes we're a nation of barbarians—but her father was half Polish and this land rightfully belongs to her. You can wear your good green dress, Danusha, and that cloak your count gave you. You'll look as fancy as the noblewomen in the procession."

The following day Danusha's father came to the kitchen house, something he'd done only rarely in the two years past. Janko hunkered on the floor to play with Adam, stroking the boy's dark hair. He glanced up at Danusha.

"I suppose you're going to see the new queen, aren't you?" he asked.

"I certainly want to. Kasia told me that everyone from the manor was allowed to go. Isn't that true?"

"Yes, we're all to have the day off," Janko said. "Pan Lucas said for us to wash ourselves and wear our best clothes, as if we had any to choose from." He picked up Adam and sat the child on his knee. "Your mother and I would be pleased if you'd walk through the woods with us, and with your brothers and sisters. We feel that the whole family should go together to see the queen."

Danusha was touched. "Of course I'll go with the family, Pappa, if you want me."

"We do, daughter. And Adam too. We can take turns carrying him—it's too far for his little legs to walk the whole way."

"No, Pappa, not Adam. He'll stay here with Kasia. You know why."

Janko traced his finger over the boy's cheek. "You guard Adam too closely," he told her. "It's not good for you or the boy either. Sooner or later people will have to see him. People will be curious about his teeth at first, and gossip a bit, but they'll get used to it soon enough. Such gossip always dies down, given enough time."

"They still talk about me, don't they, Pappa?"

"Only because you hold yourself apart from them. They think that because you spent that short time with the nobleman and bore his child, you consider yourself too fine to be with common folk."

44

"That's not true, Pappa! I don't feel that way at all," Danusha protested.

"You asked if people gossip, and I've told you," Janko said. "If you come tomorrow and bring Adam, they'll warm to you soon enough."

"I'll come tomorrow, and I'll be friendly to everyone, but I won't bring Adam." Danusha was unyielding. "I'm not going to give anyone a chance to make jest of my little boy."

"One day you may regret it, daughter," Janko said, getting to his feet. "People love to invent stories, you know. The more you hide Adam, the more they'll think that something is really strange about him. What people don't know about, they make up tales about."

She walked with him to the door. "At daybreak, Pappa. I'll meet you in the courtyard."

He paused at the door and turned to her. "Danusha, don't wear your fine clothes. Dress like the rest of us. It will be better that way."

Kasia was annoyed the next morning when Danusha put on her work dress. "Here you have the chance to look like a fine lady," she said, her voice querulous, "and you choose to look like a kitchen scullion."

"You know, Kasia, I think you're right. Help me to change into my good clothes. I own them rightfully, why shouldn't I wear them?" Danusha slipped out of her worn work dress and shook out the dark green wool, which she had stored wrapped in linen with rose petals scattered through it to keep out the smell of the kitchen. Though it was a bit tighter across the breast, it fell in perfect folds from her waist. "Give me my cloak too, Kasia. It must be cold out this morning—there was a skim of ice on the bucket outside the door."

"Now you look nice." Kasia's smile of approval was lost in her wrinkles.

"Why shouldn't I, Kasia? I'm only eighteen, though sometimes I feel the same age as you."

45

"Hah! Trying to find out my age again, are you, dearie? Well, I told you I don't know what it is. If you think we're the same age, then I must be eighteen too."

Danusha squeezed Kasia's hand and kissed Adam. "Be a good boy, and mind Kasia till Mamma gets home."

"He's always good for me," Kasia said. "He thinks I'm his grandmam."

Danusha waved at her son, then walked on light feet through the door. Although her father frowned when he saw what she was wearing, it was too joyous an occasion for anyone to stay vexed for very long.

They set out together through the fields and then into the forest, Danusha feeling pleased to be a part of the life on the manor once again as she walked with her brothers and sisters behind her parents. The younger ones acted shy with her; Stanek had been only four and Sophia six when Danusha left home. She talked to them gently and joked with them until they took her hands and begged her to tell them about the new queen. Danusha had learned more from Kasia than most of the other serfs knew.

"Jadwiga is just a girl, only eleven years old—that's not so many years older than the two of you," Danusha said. "But she is tall for her age, as tall as a woman. She was married when she was only five years old to Prince William of Austria."

"Married!" Sophia exclaimed. "Does she have a baby?"

"No, the marriage was only a ceremony, not a real marriage. Lots of kings have their children married young. It's for politics."

"What are politics?" Stanek asked.

"Oh, it's like all the quarreling that's gone on over who will rule us. But now Jadwiga is to be our queen. I suppose that when she's old enough, Prince William will come here and really be her husband. She'll need a king to help her rule."

Ahead of them, some of the serfs had begun a song, and

46

Danusha's family joined in. The air was cool enough that their breaths came in thin white clouds, but it was fine to be out in the open once again, Danusha thought. She remembered to smile politely at all the people around her, trying to appease her father over the clothes she wore. It was not hard to smile; the sun shone strongly, and when it had risen high enough, the autumn trees blazed with color.

At midmorning they reached the road where the queen was to pass. Pan Lucas rode his horse back and forth on the rutted earth, directing his serfs to line the road side by side so that it would look as if there were more of them. After a while they sat on the grass at the edge of the road. It was nearing midday and the queen's procession had not arrived.

Stanek was lying with his ear pressed to the ground. "Listen!" he cried. "The earth is making a noise."

Several of the men knelt to listen. "It's horses in the distance," they shouted. "The queen is coming!"

In a short time the clop of hoofs became recognizable, along with the rumble of carts. Over it all came the sharp-edged sound of a shrill trumpet. "She's coming, she's coming!" the children cried, dancing with excitement.

Some of the young men had climbed trees to see into the distance, and they shouted down to the others, "There it is! The procession is near—there's the dust it's raising."

"Everyone, listen to me!" Pan Lucas yelled. "The queen will be riding in a gilded carriage. When it draws near, all of you kneel."

Danusha's heart was beating faster; she could see joyous anticipation on all the faces near her. Though the child queen was coming from Hungary, the Poles already thought of her as their own.

At the head of the cavalcade rode an armored knight holding high the banner of Poland with its white eagle on a red field. Sunlight caught in billows of red silk as the banner fluttered. Behind rode another knight carrying a banner em-

47

broidered with the likeness of Saint Stanislaus, Poland's patron saint. Behind that was the whitest horse Danusha had ever seen, wearing a saddle inlaid with ivory, but it had no rider. "That's the queen's horse," Pan Lucas told his serfs. "She rides it when she isn't in her carriage."

Next came endless rows of mounted noblemen, four abreast, dressed in brilliant colors—scarlet, green, violet, blue. Over armor, each wore a surcoat emblazoned with his coat of arms. Matching pennants fluttered from their lances, and some of the men carried falcons on their wrists. Pan Lucas's serfs were awestruck at the richness of the lords' trappings—silver spurs, sword hilts encrusted with jewels, horses caparisoned in colors to match their riders'. Pan Lucas took his place at the end of the line of nobles and rode off with them, raising his head proudly as he passed his grinning serfs.

The lords were followed by a large group of young people—boys and girls—all dressed in white, holding branches in their hands and singing as they walked. They must have been trained singers because their voices blended harmoniously in the clear autumn air. At the start of each verse a trumpeter would accompany them, then break off when they reached the chorus. The serfs had never heard anything like it, and they turned to nod at one another in appreciation.

"Drop to your knees!" Danusha's father shouted. "The queen's carriage is coming."

Janko had no need to tell them. As they saw the queen's gilded conveyance roll toward them, all the serfs were filled with such awe that they knelt instinctively. The sun shone so brightly on the gold sides of the carriage that they had to shade their eyes to see the queen inside.

Young Jadwiga's eyes were huge and dark; they looked very tired. Her skin was a warm rose color, more deeply hued than the fairer Polish noblemen who rode before and after the

48

royal carriage. A silver tiara rose above her curling brown hair, which fell down over the shoulders of her blue velvet cape embroidered with the gold lilies of France. When she turned to smile at the serfs lining the road, she seemed to look straight into Danusha's eyes.

Danusha felt her own eyes fill with tears of reverence for the beautiful queen. She blinked to clear her vision, then got to her feet to see inside the heavy carts that followed next.

The carts were filled with treasures the queen had brought with her from Hungary, and with more treasures presented to her by the Polish lords at the border. Open chests showed rugs and embroideries, silver chalices and gold ewers, gleaming jewels and patterned altar vestments. A hush fell over the crowd as so much wealth rolled by; some of the peasants half reached as though they wanted to touch it. The contents of even one of the chests could have bought a hundred serfs like them.

Danusha straightened, peering down the road, not sure whether she could believe what she saw. Another mounted contingent of knights was approaching, their thin steel helmets decorated with peacock feathers. She ran along the road to where she could see the back of the first knight in the contingent and discovered what she'd hoped to find—his white cape was marked with the black cross. They were Teutonic Knights!

Quickly she scanned the row of faces, but none of them wore a leather face helmet. Still, they might know Reinmar. "Sirs, sirs!" she cried out. "Do any of you know Count Reinmar von Galt?" She called it again and again. Couldn't any of them understand Polish?

At last one of the knights reined his horse and came to a stop beside her. "You're asking about Reinmar von Galt?"

"Yes, he's a Knight of the Cross, like you."

"Of course he is, I know him well," the man said. "Do you know him?"

"I do." Danusha was stammering in her excitement. "Can you tell me where he is?"

"Just now he's at the fortress in Marienburg, on the Nogat River. I'll be going there myself after the coronation. Do you wish me to take a message to him?"

Yes! she wanted to shout. Tell him that he has a beautiful son, who must look like him. Tell him that I still love him and want to be with him.

She said, "Please, no, thank you, sir. I would prefer that you didn't even tell him that someone asked about him."

"As you wish, Pani." The knight addressed her as though she were a noblewoman. Surprised, Danusha realized that it was because of the clothes she was wearing; she hastily hid her work-worn hands beneath her cloak.

The man smiled down at her. His look was admiring; for the occasion Danusha had allowed some of her golden hair to show beneath her wimple, and her face was highly colored from excitement. "Count Reinmar is fortunate to have such a lovely lady inquiring for him, but I'll keep your secret, Pani. I promise." He spurred his horse and galloped forward to regain his place in the procession.

Hardly aware that she was moving, Danusha backed to the edge of the road and sat down while she tried to regain her composure. The last of the cavalcade had passed, but the serfs were still cheering. They wouldn't stop until the queen's party could no longer be seen in the distance.

"He's in Marienburg, beside the Nogat River," Danusha whispered. She hadn't any idea where that was, but it didn't matter. Just hearing his name spoken again had added immense joy to that unforgettable day.

Chapter 7 / *September, 1385*

"I meant for you to marry Rydek three years ago, before you went off with Count Reinmar," Pan Lucas told Danusha. "Then I forgot about it. Rydek is still unmarried, needing a woman badly from the looks of him. A big man like that ought to be able to sire a lot of sons, and you've already proven that you can bear sons. I never learned who fathered your child. Was it Count Reinmar or Squire What's-His-Name?"

"Count Reinmar," Danusha muttered, keeping her eyes down to conceal the anger in them. "Marek was only seventeen."

"Hah! That's old enough. By the time I was seventeen, I'd fathered plenty of brats in the fields around here. But it was Count Reinmar, you say?" Pan Lucas chuckled. "So much for his celibacy."

Danusha breathed deeply to control her voice. "Why must I marry, Pan Lucas? I'm content to work in the kitchen house. Kasia needs me. She can no longer stand on her feet for very long."

"Who said anything about your leaving the kitchen? You'll work there the same as usual, but you'll spend your nights in Rydek's bed. I don't care what you do as long as you produce serfs for the manor." Pan Lucas tilted his head and pulled on his beard, studying her face. "Why so downcast? Listen, woman, I'll be generous. Rydek can eat his meals in the kitchen house so you won't have to cook for him when you go home at night. There, what do you say to that? I always treat my serfs well."

"Please, Pan Lucas. I don't want to marry."

"You'll do as I say. The priest is coming tomorrow to offer prayers at the harvest festival. He can marry you then. Rydek is a good-looking fellow for a serf. You should be glad to get him. Now go back to work and don't look so woebegone or you'll make me wroth."

After Pan Lucas had left, Danusha leaned her head against the stone hearth, weighted with despair. The last thing she ever wanted was to marry; her love had been given once, and it could never be given again. Yet she was obliged to do whatever Pan Lucas ordered.

She thought of the young queen, Jadwiga. It was said that her true love, Prince William, had arrived in Krakow in August to consummate the marriage. But the Polish lords had locked William out of the castle and connived to make the queen marry Jagiello, a pagan lord three times her age. If even a queen could be forced to marry against her wishes, what hope was there for a serf?

Danusha stood next to Rydek on the packed earth of the manor courtyard. Behind them the rest of the serfs waited in a solemn group—Danusha's parents, her brothers and sisters, Rydek's mother, the widow Riska, and the dozen or so other families who belonged to Pan Lucas. The manor lord himself stood arguing with the priest over what fee would have to be paid. Pan Lucas wanted the cleric to perform a baptism as well as the wedding for no extra charge, but the priest said he should be paid twice for administering two sacraments. While the argument went on, the serfs shuffled their feet and stole glances at the bridal couple.

Danusha wore no garland in her hair; since she was no longer a maiden, she had no right to the bridal wreath. She wouldn't have bothered to wear her good green dress if Kasia had not convinced her that she would shame her parents by appearing in her stained work dress. Rydek stood scowling; it was evident to Danusha that he had not wanted the wedding any more than she had.

She turned to glance at her mother. For once the hurt was gone from the older woman's face; she looked relieved. Danusha knew what her mother must be thinking: after a few more years, with Danusha safely wedded, gossip about the bastard son would die down.

Adam held old Kasia's hand, pulling on it as he chattered. At two he talked as well as a three-year-old. Many of the serf women had shown surprise at his precociousness; for most of them it was the first time they'd had a look at him. Danusha was thankful that in the gray dusk of the autumn evening, his teeth wouldn't show.

"All right, kneel down," the priest said abruptly. He began the ceremony that would unite Danusha to Rydek, speaking the words rapidly, his tone still irked after the quarrel with Pan Lucas.

Danusha's face felt rigid as stone; her heart, too, felt like a stone inside her. She tried not to hear the priest's words but they went on relentlessly. She could sense Rydek's stiffness as he knelt beside her. Danusha had hardly known him in the past years. He was more of a stranger to her than he'd been in the time before she went away, and even then she'd never given him much thought.

Two candles had been set on stones to create some semblance of an altar. They cast moving shadows over the faces of the priest and the bridal couple, but of a sudden, a gust of breeze made one of the candle flames dance wildly and then sputter out. A gasp rose from the crowd of onlookers at such an omen, which meant that either the bride or groom faced an untimely death before long.

The priest's black brows drew together as his mouth turned

down; all the old superstitions irritated him, and he was already vexed with Pan Lucas. He ended the ceremony brusquely, uttering an "Amen" which sounded more like a rebuke than a benediction.

A ragged, half-hearted cheer went up from the gathering of serfs. No one seemed very happy except for Danusha's mother, who came to kiss her. "Now you can wear the coif of a lawfully wedded wife," she whispered, with a barely concealed look of triumph. "And little Adam will have a father."

"He has a father, a better man than this one," Danusha whispered back, but nothing could dim her mother's satisfaction.

When the harvest festival began, everyone seemed to forget the bridal couple. Rydek was the first one at the wine vat.

"Danusha," Kasia said, coming up to her, "let Adam stay with me for the next few nights. You know how it is with bridegrooms—they're insatiable at first. Adam is so bright he'd notice."

"Yes, Kasia, keep him tonight," Danusha agreed. "If he asks where I am, tell him he'll see me early in the morning."

The festival went on for hours while the bright moon climbed higher in the sky. Kasia took Adam home to bed, but Rydek stayed next to the wine vat emptying one cup after another. The strong wine only seemed to make him more morose.

At last it was time for the bridal couple to be led to bed. It wasn't necessary for Danusha to pretend reluctance the way a young maid was supposed to on her wedding night; she was far more reluctant than any virgin could have been. Rydek stumbled as he walked, supported by some of the other men. It was a strangely somber procession for a wedding party.

The hut they'd been given was an old one, unused for a long time. It smelled musty, even though Danusha had tried to air it the day before. They stopped at the doorway. The other serfs didn't lead them inside, as was the custom, but

54

stayed outside. The usual bridal-night jests were left unspoken.

Someone had attached a piece of black cloth and a wreath made of straw just inside the door frame, a sign that the bride was not chaste. Danusha bit her lip as she pulled them down, but Rydek was too drunk to notice.

He fell heavily to the pallet on the floor. For a long time Danusha stood quietly near the door, hoping that he would sleep deeply in his drunkenness. At last, without removing her dress, she lowered herself cautiously to the pallet.

But Rydek was not as drunk as he seemed. After he had taken her, as was his right, he began to sob. "You weren't a virgin," he cried. "I wanted a virgin for a bride."

"Of course I was not a virgin," she said scornfully. "You know I have a son. Only one virgin has ever before had a son, and I am not she."

His fist caught her across the mouth. "Don't ever talk to me in that manner," he yelled, "as though you were the one wronged. I have been wronged! I had to take you as my wife, and your whoreson with you."

Danusha grabbed him by the hair. "Never call Adam that name!" she screamed, pounding Rydek's head against the floor. "If you dare call him that again, I'll . . ."

"You'll what?" Rydek's weight was heavy on her as he slapped her face. "You'll keep that mouth of yours shut fast if you know what's good for you."

Seething with fury, Danusha remained quiet until at last Rydek slept. Then she crept from the hut and returned to the kitchen house.

Danusha spent her nights in the cottage, but she stayed in the kitchen house from dawn until after Rydek took his evening meals there. While Rydek ate, Adam hid cowering in the storage alcove as Kasia shot looks of hatred at the man. Because he was big, and brutal when drunk, even Kasia

55

sheathed her acid tongue in Rydek's presence. And since he became furious if he caught so much as a glimpse of Adam, it seemed best to let the boy remain with Kasia. Thus Rydek never learned of Adam's abnormalities.

All too soon Danusha realized that she was with child again. The knowledge filled her with dread because she worried that she would feel dislike for Rydek's child when it was born. She and Rydek shared a barely concealed hostility; seldom did they speak more than half a dozen words in the night. Yet they shared the same bed. To do otherwise would have marked Danusha as a woman beyond redemption. She didn't care, but Rydek insisted that since they were wed, she had to act like a wife.

When the new baby was born, Danusha named him Marcin and was relieved to discover that she loved him as she loved Adam. Perhaps not quite so much, because Marcin was perfect and didn't need the fierce protectiveness Danusha lavished over Adam. As it happened, the arrival of Marcin turned out to be a blessing.

Adam had been growing more and more fretful at his confinement in the kitchen house and had spent much time lying flat beside the door to peer through the crack beneath it at the world outside. This action always irked Danusha, but she said nothing about it. Better to have him spy that way than to run outside, she thought.

After Marcin's birth Adam took delight in amusing and being amused by his baby brother. He treated Marcin as a playmate from the very first and no longer bothered to peer underneath the door. When blond Marcin grew old enough to toddle around the kitchen, Adam watched over him with a patience that surprised both Danusha and Kasia. He always guarded the baby closely so that he shouldn't stumble near the fire in the hearth.

On the feast day of Saint Luke, October 18, Danusha stayed late in the kitchen house scouring the iron cauldron. Because it was Pan Lucas's name day, he'd given the serfs a barrel of wine for them to drink in celebration. Danusha knew that Rydek must be drinking heavily; he hadn't bothered to come for his evening meal.

She looked up in surprise as her father threw open the kitchen door. "Come at once," Janko told her. "There's trouble."

Alarmed, Danusha put down the cauldron and went to wash the soot from her hands.

"Let that go. Don't take time to clean yourself," Janko shouted. "There was a fight and Rydek is wounded. He's in your cottage."

As they hurried to cross the courtyard, Janko spoke to her hastily in broken phrases. "They were drinking, the bunch of them. Some quarrel came up . . . Rydek's fault. He'd been insisting that you were a virgin when he married you. The others laughed at him. Rydek got furious and went after one of the men. With a scythe. To save himself, the man took a pitchfork and threw it at Rydek. He's bleeding badly."

The serfs, standing in a little knot around the door of Danusha's hut, fell back to let her pass. One of the women hissed at her.

Horrified, feeling sick with helplessness, Danusha knelt beside their pallet, pressing wet cloths against the three gaping wounds in Rydek's stomach. In less than an hour he was dead.

Chapter 8 / *Harvest 1388*

If Danusha had avoided the manor serfs before, after Rydek's death she avoided them even more. They seemed to blame her for his death. After all, they reasoned, if Danusha had been a virgin, none of that would have happened, would it? Rydek had been so grieved over having to wed a women with a bastard child that his mind got addled, and he tried to pretend that Danusha *was* a virgin when she married him. Since that had led to his death, it was Danusha's fault.

Danusha never bothered to defend herself. "Let them say what they want to say," she told Kasia angrily. "Why should I care what they say? I won't listen to their gossip, and I don't want you to repeat any more of it to me."

Kasia's forehead creased in disapproval as she answered, "You're wrong in this, Danusha. It's not wise to be on bad terms with kin and workmates. You're as stubborn as a mule, and don't forget, the only reward a mule gets for his balkiness is a painful beating."

Danusha refused to be persuaded. She hardly ever left the kitchen house, and then only at night to take the boys out for fresh air.

She was not happy, but she was not so very unhappy, either. She was free of Rydek, and her sons gave purpose to her life.

Two-year-old Marcin was a handsome child, big for his

58

age, but as slow to talk as Adam had been fast. Marcin possessed a placid nature, deliberating over every action for a long while before he performed it.

Adam, at five, was as quick as a hummingbird. He darted around the kitchen pretending to be a horseman, so that Danusha often had to scold him for running into Kasia's legs. He made up long, fanciful stories to amuse Marcin, and if Marcin paid little attention to them, Adam made up songs instead.

One day in late August Pan Lucas pounded on the kitchen door and called for Danusha to come outside.

"We're short-handed in the fields," he told her. "I want you to help with the harvest this year, Danusha. The old woman Kasia can manage the kitchen by herself for a month or so."

"Pan Lucas, Kasia is becoming so feeble . . ." Danusha began. Then her face brightened. "But my Adam can help her. He can't lift the pot off the spit, but he can fetch everything else so that Kasia won't have to move around much."

"How old is that boy now?" Pan Lucas asked.

"He's five."

"Then bring him to the fields, too. He can carry water for the laborers."

"Pan Lucas!"

He grew annoyed. "What are you objecting to, woman? All serfs start work at five, either tending younger children or carrying water, as your son will do. Is there any reason why he should be treated different?"

Danusha lowered her head, unable to think of an answer that would sound reasonable to her master. "No, Pan Lucas. I'll come to the fields tomorrow with my sons."

It was good to be out under the sky, under the hot sun that burned into her back. It was good to feel earth under her bare feet again. Danusha swung her scythe rhythmically at the

59

silver-tipped stalks of barley, pausing every few minutes to look around for her boys. They ran across the stubbled furrows, Adam whooping with the freedom of being outdoors, Marcin stumbling as he tried to run after his big brother. Their faces flushed with heat and exertion, and their damp hair clung to their foreheads. As she watched her handsome sons at play, Danusha felt pride surge and swell within her until she could scarcely draw her breath.

After they'd had their fill of running, the boys looked wistfully at the other children; Danusha had warned them to stay at a distance from anyone in the fields. Once, at midmorning, she saw Adam walk toward a little girl his own age. He was holding out a wildflower. Danusha dropped her scythe and ran after him, pulling him back.

The girl's mother flushed with resentment. "Don't go near that boy or his brother," the woman told her daughter, loudly enough to be heard across the furrows where Danusha was working. "They're not our kind of people. They put on airs to hide their wickedness."

Some of the joy went out of the day for Danusha. She was torn between wanting to let the boys play with other children and her fear that someone would notice Adam's teeth. As she swung her scythe steadily, moving from one row to another, she noticed that the other serfs were talking about her again.

When the workers called for water, Danusha dropped her scythe and carried it to them herself. No one objected, but they didn't exchange any words with her, either.

After the sun dropped low and work was finished for the day, Danusha picked up Marcin and carried him back toward the kitchen house. Adam followed, dragging the long-handled scythe. The arms and faces of both boys were burned red from the sun.

"Mamma, my skin hurts," Adam complained.

"Your skin hurts because you're sunburned, Adam. So is

Marcin. See how red he is? You look just the same. We'll stop at the well and splash cold water on both of you. That will make your skin feel better.''

When they went inside the kitchen, they found Kasia panting from the exertion of cooking. "Here, let me finish it," Danusha said. "You sit down and rest."

"No, you can't drudge out in the fields all day long and then come in here and do the kitchen work," Kasia protested.

"I'm hardly tired at all. It was so nice to be outside that I didn't mind the work, although my shoulders do ache a little. I'll get used to it. You should have seen the boys, Kasia. They so enjoyed running in the field."

Kasia settled on her stool. "Come here, Adam. Tell Kasia all about your day."

"I wanted to give a girl a flower," Adam said, "but Mamma wouldn't let me."

Kasia wasn't listening to him. "Turn your face toward me, child," she said. "What's the matter with your skin?"

"He's sunburned," Danusha explained. "Both boys are sunburned. Marcin is as red as Adam."

"But Adam is beginning to blister. Look, Danusha. Water blisters are rising on his face. His arms, too."

Danusha paused in her work. "I didn't expect his skin to be so tender. Is Marcin blistering?"

"No, only Adam. There's some goose grease on the shelf. Bring it to me, and I'll rub it on Adam's skin."

When they began to spread the thick grease over him, Adam squirmed and cried, "I don't want that on me. It smells bad and it hurts."

"Stand still to show me that you're a brave boy," Kasia crooned. "This will make you all better."

"Please don't, Kasia," Adam whimpered. "It hurts me."

"There, we're all finished. In the morning your blisters will be gone."

61

The next morning Marcin's sunburn had faded, but Adam's skin was still sore. "Strange," Kasia mused, "usually it's the fair ones who get burned by the sun, and the dark-haired ones not so much. But don't worry about it. When Adam gets used to the sun, his skin will toughen and turn brown."

The boys played again in the field while Danusha worked, but Adam moved more slowly, stopping often to rub his cheeks and arms. When Danusha examined him during the rest at midday, she discovered that some of the blisters had broken and were turning sore. "Play in the shade of the trees for the rest of the afternoon," she instructed him as she went back to work.

Adam tried to stay in the shade, but he was in charge of Marcin. Whenever Marcin ran away to chase a bird or to follow a butterfly, Adam went after him.

By the third day his skin grew worse. The bigger blisters burst and ran, leaving open sores. Slowly the sores crusted over; after a week his face and hands were covered with scabs.

"Do you think he has the pox that children get?" Danusha asked Kasia at night.

"No, he has no spots at all on his chest as he would if it were the mild pox. Anyway the sores are too big, more like the deadly pox, but he isn't sick. So it can't be either kind of pox."

"The goose grease hasn't helped at all," Danusha declared.

"So here's what you should do," Kasia told her. "Take him out tomorrow before sunrise. Gather spiderwebs laden with dew, and put those on his face and hands. That's a remedy for skin ailments I learned long ago."

In the morning Danusha did as Kasia instructed; Adam sputtered and screwed up his face in disgust as the webs clung to his mouth and chin. But that remedy didn't help, nor

62

did another Kasia concocted of wych-elm bark. Though the old scabs dried, new sores appeared on Adam's face.

A few days later, while Danusha worked in a farther field, a half-grown girl came up and tugged on her sleeve. "I'm supposed to ask you . . ." The girl looked for support from a cluster of peasant women a few furrows away. "I'm supposed to ask you, does your boy have the pox?"

"No, it isn't the pox." Danusha tried to sound reassuring. "There's something wrong with his skin, but it isn't catching. See, his brother doesn't have it."

"They want to know for sure," the girl persisted, "whether he has a fever."

"He has no fever."

Looking furtively at Danusha, the girl ran to Adam and pressed her hand against his forehead.

"My name is Adam," he said, smiling up at the stranger.

"His teeth!" The girl shrieked loudly enough to be heard the width and breadth of the field. "He has red teeth!"

Before Danusha could move to put down her scythe, a husky man who had been working the next furrow ran to seize Adam roughly, lifting him into the air. "Open your mouth, boy," he cried. "Let me see you teeth."

As Danusha reached to snatch her child from the man, he butted her roughly with his shoulder, knocking her to the ground. Before she could get to her feet, he ran across the field with Adam in his arms.

All along the furrows, serfs straightened from their work, then dropped their scythes and hurried to meet the man who was carrying the screaming Adam toward them. "What is it? Danusha's bastard has red teeth, the girl said. Come on, let's have a look."

They shoved and jostled, pushing against one another for a better look. Adam was crying so hard that his mouth was open wide as one serf after another pulled his head toward them and peered inside his mouth. "By God, they really are red!"

"Put him down!" Danusha cried, trying to fight her way through the solid wall of human bodies that surrounded Adam. She looked around for help, but her father's family had been assigned to work in the barn, and none of the field serfs would lift a finger to help her.

"Maybe he's been eating beets," a child suggested.

"Here, take a rag and wipe the teeth. See if the color comes off." One of the women forced open Adam's mouth to scrub his teeth with a dirty rag. "No, it won't come off. The red is part of his teeth."

With the strength of desperation, Danusha pushed herself toward the center of the crowd. "Let him alone, he's only a child," she screamed, reaching to snatch Adam from the man who held him, but the man pulled away, tipping Adam's head so that the others could see inside his mouth. "Please, please put him down," Danusha sobbed. "You're frightening him."

"It's no wonder the bastard has scabs on his face and has red teeth," a shrill-voiced woman cried. "His father was probably the Devil." She started to laugh at her own joke, then stopped when she realized that no one else was laughing with her.

The serfs had turned to stare at the woman, some in disbelief, some aghast and yet excited at such a horrifying possibility. The woman, when she saw that everyone's eyes were on her, tried to enhance her story. "Remember, Rydek insisted that Danusha was a virgin when he married her. Couldn't the Devil sire a child and still leave the mother a virgin?"

The man who had been holding Adam dropped him quickly and took a step backward. Danusha scooped Adam into her arms, then ran to where Marcin sat uncomprehending and bewildered. She carried both boys into the trees

64

alongside the field, sitting down to rock Adam, telling him not to be afraid, although her own heart was pounding and her cheeks were wet with tears.

"Why did they want to see my teeth, Mamma?" Adam sobbed, stammering in near hysteria. "Why did they do that to me?"

"Never mind, it doesn't matter." Danusha held him tightly, pressing his head against her breast. Within her, she felt a tearing physical pain of anguish for her son. "It's all over now, dearest. Don't cry," she soothed him in a shaking voice. Marcin leaned against her back, crying too, but when his mother paid him no heed, he sat down and began to pluck blades of grass. After a long while, Adam's sobbing subsided to hiccoughs, and then he was silent, clinging tightly to Danusha.

That evening when Danusha told Kasia about the harassment, the old woman was furious. "Ignorant serfs," she spat, "frightening an innocent boy that way!" She pulled Adam to her, taking his face in her hands to comfort him. After a moment she called, "Danusha, come here." Her voice sounded strained.

"What is it?"

"Look close. Very close."

"Look at what?"

"This." Kasia pointed. A light sprinkling of fine, downy hair was growing along Adam's forehead, cheeks, and chin between the scabbed sores. It was so light as to be almost unapparent, but Kasia's sharp eyes had seen it.

"Oh, God, no! Oh, God!" Danusha collapsed on the floor, wailing.

"Don't cry, Mamma. The bad man in the field won't take me any more," Adam said, as Kasia scolded, "Don't carry on so, Danusha. You'll upset him. It's only a little bit of hair. No one will even notice it."

"They'll notice," Danusha cried. "They'll be watching him more closely now. They'll look for anything unusual about him."

"Then don't take him into the fields," Kasia urged. "Leave him here with me."

"I have to take him. Each day Pan Lucas comes to see how the work is going. Twice he's asked me whether Adam is carrying the water, and I lied, saying he was. Pan Lucas wants him to work."

Kasia was silent, rocking Adam against her. Then she whispered, "If you must take him, you'd best keep him beside you at all times."

Danusha wiped her eyes and leaned against Kasia, too exhausted by the agonies of the day to weep any more. "I know why this is happening," she said, her voice guttural. "It's a punishment because I sinned with Reinmar. Because I loved him. But, oh, God! why are you punishing my baby instead of me?" She laughed bitterly. "No, God knows best, doesn't he? He can hurt me more by doing these things to Adam."

"Hush, Danusha. Hush!" Kasia reached to embrace Danusha, holding both mother and son against her bony body. The old woman moved her lips as though she wanted to offer words of comfort, but could think of none that would console and yet be truthful.

After Adam's torment, the serfs ignored Danusha and her sons, looking past them as if they didn't exist. From that time on, the water was carried by another child who had been chosen by the serfs themselves.

In the weeks afterward Danusha stayed as far away from the others as she could manage, always working the furrows on the edges of the fields closest to the woods. The reaping was nearly finished; if she could keep the boys away from the curious serfs for only another day or two, they would be safe in the kitchen house once more.

Adam had recovered from his fright but was wary, calling to his brother to come back whenever Marcin tried to move closer to the other children. When Marcin wouldn't come, Adam ran after him and pulled him back to the shelter of the trees.

The dried scabs on Adam's face fell off but left disfiguring scars, and whenever he was in the sun, new blisters formed. The hair on his face grew a bit thicker and darker, resembling the soft down found on the backs of some newborn infants.

It was the last day of harvest when Adam ran to Danusha, crying so hard he could scarcely talk.

"What is it, Adam?" she asked, alarmed.

"Mamma," he gasped, "I went int . . . into the woods. I had to make water, and you told me . . . to always be by myself when I make water. But Mamma, I didn't know . . . there was another boy in the woods. He saw me make water. He asked why was my water red, and I said I didn't know. He said he was going to tell the other people."

Danusha's heart sank. "Which boy was it?"

"That one over there. In the long shirt."

She could see the older boy excitedly telling his story to a little knot of serfs. As he spoke, the serfs called others to join the group, until every peasant in the field was clustered around the boy.

Danusha stood at the far end of the row pressing her two sons against her skirt. Half a field of standing grain separated her from the group of twenty or more serfs. In the other part of the field, grain already cut lay scattered on the ground or stood partially bound into sheaves abandoned by the serfs in their haste to partake of the excitement.

Danusha waited, frightened, to learn what they would do. She could see them arguing and gesturing among themselves,

67

but their voices didn't carry over the distance separating them from her. If they tried to harm her, she would run, but she knew that she could never escape them while carrying Marcin in her arms and dragging Adam by the hand.

The impasse seemed to last forever. At last the peasant group broke up, and the workers went back to reaping. Letting out her breath slowly, Danusha bent to pick up her scythe.

She was cutting grain when the first clod of dirt hit her.

"Whore!" a shrill voice screamed behind her. Danusha whirled to confront the scrawny woman who had said that Adam was the Devil's son. Circled around her were other women, among them Rydek's mother, whose face wore a look of hatred. Behind them, the men leaned on their scythes, grinning as they urged the women on with jeers and whistles.

"Adam, Marcin," Danusha murmured, "stand behind Mamma and don't move. Adam, hold Marcin's hand."

The next clod of earth hit her on the cheek. "Devil slut!" a heavy-set woman yelled. "Slept with the Devil and begot the Devil's brat. Stand aside, Danusha, and let us see your devil bastard make red water."

"Yes, tell him to make water for us," all of them shouted.

Keeping her eyes steady on the crowd, Danusha lifted the scythe above her head. "If any one of you moves toward my sons, I'll cut you open," she threatened, her voice harsh with fury.

The men laughed and yelled while the women let loose a barrage of stones. Most of the stones were thrown wide, although a few of them stung Danusha. She held her ground, raising the scythe higher, but when the women began to press forward yelling obscenities, she threw the scythe toward them, picking up the boys to run into the woods. A few of the serfs attempted to follow her, but the shrill woman cried out anxiously, "Don't go in there. If the child really is

68

half-devil, you wouldn't want to be caught in the woods with him!''

Danusha ran until she had to stop and rest. Panting, she dropped on the ground to decide what to do, while she held the frightened boys against her. One thing was certain, she wouldn't go back into the field. And she couldn't stay on the manor. She didn't believe the serfs would really harm her— yet! But she was a serf herself, and she knew how their minds worked. They were not usually malicious, but they led dull lives. Any uncommon incident was inevitably dramatized to enliven the tedium of their days. The idea that Adam had a devil-father was now partly a joke, partly tantalizing speculation. Yet as soon as the next serf had a bit of bad luck—a cow that died or a horse that went lame—he would look suspiciously at Adam and wonder if the boy had cast a spell. Winter idleness would provide time for rumor and accusation, and when a child died of croup or pox, Adam would be blamed. The serfs were likely to rouse one another until one of them grabbed a knife and shouted, "It is our duty to protect our families! Let's kill the devil-child!"

Danusha was not going to wait for that to happen. She took both whimpering boys by the hand and circled back toward the manor house, staying in the woods as long as possible. When she entered the courtyard, she stepped forward hesitantly, but the yard was deserted in the late September sunshine.

"Kasia!" Inside the kitchen she awakened the old woman from a doze. "Kasia, we have to leave."

"What? Who's leaving?"

"I'm going to take the boys and go away from here. They stoned us in the fields this afternoon."

Kasia dropped her head to her hands. "I knew it would happen. I knew it. Where will you go?"

"There's only one place I can think of—the monastery near Krol Forest. When the monks brought me down from the

Tatra Mountains, they were kind to me. If I explain to them what has happened, they might let me work in the monastery."

"That means you'll be a runaway serf, Danusha."

"Kasia, no one will know where I am except you."

"Leave it to me, then. I'll lead them all on a merry chase, believe me." Kasia's eyes filled with grief as she hugged the boys to her. "I'll never see you again, my sweet little Marcin and my beautiful Adam . . ." Her words faltered as she caught Danusha's eye. Both of them knew that Adam was no longer beautiful.

Chapter 9

O f course, I remember you," Brother Vincenty told her.
"We brought you and the lame horse down from the
mountain after the storm. The horse is fine now, we use it for
plowing. Let's see, how long ago was that? Four years?"

"Six years, Brother Vincenty."

"So these are your sons? That blond one is a handsome
fellow." Brother Vincenty smiled at Marcin, but his eyes
brushed past Adam's scarred face.

"We've come here because we . . . I . . . wondered if you
could let me stay and work at the monastery. I can do field
work, and I can cook," Danusha said. "I'm a good cook. I've
worked in Pan Lucas's kitchen ever since you brought me
back."

Brother Vincenty appeared bewildered. "Then why are you
asking to come here? Don't you belong to Pan Lucas?"

Danusha breathed unevenly, wondering how to begin. She
was worn out from the two-day journey with the little boys,
but she had to explain her troubles in just the right way so
that the monk wouldn't send her off.

"Here, Danusha," he said kindly, "come sit on this bench
in the courtyard. I'll fetch you some water to drink. You, boy,
what's your name? Adam? See over there in the orchard?
There are a few apples left on the trees. Can you climb up and
get some for you and your brother? That's right, stay in the

orchard for a little while so that your mother can talk to me."

Brother Vincenty handed her a cup of water, then sat next to her. "I can see that you're troubled, Danusha," he said. "I am not a priest, so I can't hear your confession, if that's what you want."

"No, Brother Vincenty, I just need a place to stay." Slowly, painfully, she told him about being stoned in the field.

"I don't understand how such a thing could have happened," he said. "Where was your husband while this was going on?"

"My husband is dead. Brother Vincenty, I want you to know from the very first, before you decide what to do with me . . . my husband Rydek was the father only of Marcin. Adam is Count Reinmar's son."

The monk stared at her. "When was Adam born?"

"In the June after I returned to the manor."

The monk moved his fingers, and Danusha would have smiled if she weren't so apprehensive. It was obvious that he was counting the months between the time he saw her with Reinmar and the time of Adam's birth. After a moment he said, "So that explains why the boys look nothing alike. I must say that I feel outrage that Count Reinmar should have used you the way he did. He has taken holy vows to remain celibate! Did he know that you were pregnant when he sent you back?"

"I didn't know it myself until after I returned to the manor. He knows nothing about it."

"Then I shall send a message to the Teutonic Order at Marienburg telling Count Reinmar that he has an obligation to care for his son."

"No, don't do that! Please, Brother Vincenty, I can care for Adam myself. I didn't come here for that kind of help. I'll go now." Danusha stood and picked up the bundle of clothes she'd brought with her.

"Sit down, woman." Brother Vincenty took her arm and pulled her back to the bench. For a while he chewed his thumbnail and watched the boys in the orchard. "You have a forgiving nature, evidently," he said finally. "It's true that if news got out that Count Reinmar has a child, it could harm him. He's rising higher and higher in the ranks of the Teutonic Order, though he's something of a mysterious figure with his face and hands always covered." Brother Vincenty turned to Danusha in wonder. "So *that's* why he covers his face! He has the same disfigurement as your son Adam!"

"I suspect so," she answered, looking down.

"Well, well!" The monk put his pudgy hands on his knees. He'd grown much heavier since Danusha last saw him, but the extra weight seemed to add to his attitude of authority. "You know you're a runaway serf, Danusha. To tell the truth, I've never had much love for Pan Lucas, but we can't keep you here in the monastery. No women are allowed inside, especially one as young and pretty as you. But let me talk to the abbot. Something might be arranged."

Danusha looked at him with hope. "Brother Vincenty, I'm a hard worker. Whatever work you can find for me, I'll do it gladly, even the most menial tasks. Adam can already help some, and in a few years Marcin will be able to work."

"There, there, Danusha." The monk patted her hand. "We won't throw you out to starve with your sons. I'll go now and bring you something to eat. You'll have to sleep in the stable tonight with your boys—our guest house burned down some years ago and we've never replaced it."

Danusha smiled. "I slept in your stable once before," she said. It seemed to her that a thousand years had passed since then.

In the morning she was up and had washed both boys at the well before Brother Vincenty appeared, although it was

73

still early. The courtyard was as cold as she remembered it from the time before; she was glad that this time she wore shoes.

"God be with you, Danusha," Brother Vincenty said. "I've spoken to the abbot about you. The abbot hasn't much love for Pan Lucas, either—we've been quarreling with him for years over a piece of property. Come and sit down; I don't like to stand when I can be sitting."

Brother Vincenty arranged his bulk on the bench and waited for Danusha to join him. She was nervous, but as she studied his face and noticed that his expression seemed genial, she felt somewhat heartened.

"You know we possess all the land around here," he began. "No, you probably don't know that, but it does belong to us. Most of Krol Forest. This monastery has been in existence for almost two hundred years. As the neighboring lords die, they bequeath bits of land to us in return for masses said for their souls. Well, that isn't important. As it happens, we own a little cottage deep in the forest. It was lived in by an old woodcutter until a few years ago when he died; since then the cottage has been vacant. Last night the abbot gave his permission for you to live in the cottage with your sons."

"Oh, Brother Vincenty! . . ." Danusha seized his hand in gratitude.

"There . . . it's all right." The monk looked embarrassed. "The land around the cottage used to be cleared, although it may have become overgrown in the past few years. You can plant a garden, and there's a stream nearby full of fish. After your sons are big enough, they can chop wood and bring it to the monastery, but for the time being, we'll be content to have you keep the place in good repair."

Tears of relief began spilling over Danusha's cheeks. "I can chop wood myself, right now," she said. "You won't have to wait until the boys are grown."

"That won't be necessary, Danusha," Brother Vincenty told

74

her. "After all, it is God's work to help people in need. Allow us monks that satisfaction. And . . . um . . .," he cleared his throat. "From time to time you'll want things—cloth and leather to make clothes for the boys, perhaps pots or needles. A few times each year a group of the brothers goes to the market at Wieliczka for supplies. We will provide you with whatever you need."

"You don't have to, Brother Vincenty. I have money."

"You do?"

Danusha unwrapped her bundle of clothes and took out a cloth tied into a knot. When she untied it and spread it out for Brother Vincenty to see, the monk looked startled.

"Where did you get so much money?" he asked. "They're gold and silver coins!"

"Count Reinmar gave them to me before he left me," she said. "I've never used any of it because I didn't need anything." Curious, she fingered the coins. "Is it a great deal of wealth, Brother Vincenty?"

"For a king it wouldn't make up much of his treasury, but for common folk it's a great deal. It will be enough to keep you comfortable, if you use it wisely, until your boys are grown to manhood."

Danusha piled the money in her lap, pleased that she would not have to depend on the charity of the monks. "I didn't realize how much they were worth," she said. "On the manor the serfs never get paid in coin."

"Wrap it up and put it in a safe place," Brother Vincenty told her. "Then call your boys, and I'll take you to the cottage. It's a two-mile walk." He looked ruefully at his fat stomach. "But the exercise will do me good."

Danusha was elated over the cottage. It was not large, but it was well built and had a hearth with a real chimney—the woodcutter must have known how to work with stone. At Pan Lucas's manor only the great hall had a hearth with a chimney; all the other hearths were beneath smoke vents, which were opened and closed with long poles.

"We've kept everything just as it was when the old wood-cutter died," Brother Vincenty explained, "hoping we'd find someone to take his place. It was good fortune for you, my girl, that we didn't search too hard. See, there are his axes, his long bow, and a net for fishing."

"And an iron pot, wooden trenchers, and spoons," Danusha exclaimed with pleasure.

"Even a wooden chest he was carving before he died," the monk pointed out.

The room was filled with dust and cobwebs and with bits of daub that had fallen from between the timbers. In a week Danusha had it clean and repaired. At first the cottage was somewhat drafty, but she continued, until the clay from the creek banks had frozen solid, to plaster daub on the inside walls, making them tight against winter winds.

She had insisted on paying the monks for the sacks of grain and salt they carried out to last her through the winter. While Krol Forest was deep in snow, Brother Vincenty would be unable to visit her. Through what remained of the autumn, Danusha caught fish and salted them, picked mushrooms and strung them to dry, and with the boys' help, gathered nuts and wild onions from the forest.

When winter came, the isolation sometimes made her rest-less and irritable, especially when Adam and Marcin grew fretful and quarreled. Often she found herself reacting with unreasonable wrath to whatever small mischiefs the boys got into, and when that happened, she threw on her cloak and went out to stand on the path which had been cleared from the cottage to the privy, stamping her feet until her temper grew cooler. Once near Christmas when she was outside pac-ing the frozen ground, she heard the sound of bells from the monastery chapel, borne faintly to her on the thin, icy air. Immediately she felt shame for her anger, and dropped to her knees in the snow to thank God that he had led her to a place where Adam could be safe.

After the last snow had melted and the days grew warm enough, Danusha dug a garden, setting out plants Brother Vincenty had carried to her during several of his visits. On a day when the garden had greened with the tops of onions and turnips, Danusha was on her knees pulling weeds from around her cabbage plants. Hearing a noise along the forest path, she straightened abruptly.

It wasn't Adam or Marcin; they were beside her helping to weed. Yet it sounded too loud for Brother Vincenty. Fallen branches were cracking with a sharp noise, as though something heavy trod on them. "Adam, Marcin," she said quietly, "go into the cottage and stay there until I tell you to come out."

Adam picked up Marcin and carried him inside as Danusha got to her feet. She waited, brushing the soil from her hands as she peered anxiously through the trees. It seemed that a large animal was picking its way along the path, yet there were no bears in this part of the forest, and the monks didn't own horses for riding, only for farm work.

"Danusha, is that you up ahead?" a familiar voice called.

Danusha almost fell in her haste to reach the entrance of the forest path. "Kasia!" she screamed. "Kasia, how did you get here?"

The old woman was sitting astride a donkey, her withered legs sticking out beneath drawn-up skirts. Danusha threw her arms around Kasia, nearly knocking her off the donkey. "How did you get here? When did you . . . what are . . .?" she cried, nearly unable to speak in her delight.

"Well, gracious God, lead this beast to your cottage and help me off it. My poor backside isn't used to such a jarring. Where's Adam? Where's Marcin?"

"Boys! Come out!" Danusha shrieked. "See who's here!"

Danusha lifted Kasia from the donkey and set the old

woman on a tree stump near the door of the cottage. The boys were all over her, squealing as they hugged her, patting her hands and her sunken cheeks. After she'd exclaimed over how much they'd grown, Kasia made Danusha sit beside her.

"Now I'll tell you all that has happened," Kasia said, "and then I must lie down because I'm so weary. To begin with, Pan Lucas died a week ago. Yes, he's gone to meet the saints, or more likely in the other direction, if you ask me. The manor is all in an uproar because he's left no heir—no legitimate one, that is. So the estate reverts to the crown, but for now, there's no one in charge." She paused to catch her breath after such a rush of words.

"Then I said to myself," she continued, speaking more slowly, "why am I waiting here for whoever comes to be the next lord? I had a few coins tucked away . . ." Kasia's sharp eyes glittered. "You didn't know that, did you, dearie? Yes, I had a bit tucked away just as you did. It's hidden here, where my bosom used to be. So I went to the stable one night and took this miserable donkey—Pan Lucas owed me that much, for sure—and I started out without letting anyone see me. And here I am, mighty sore in the bones, and as tired as a sow with fourteen piglets."

"Dear Kasia!" Danusha couldn't get enough of looking at the old woman. "How did you find our cottage?"

"When I arrived at the monastery, I talked to the monk, the fat one. He directed me here. And here I'll stay, till I die, if you'll have me."

"Have you!" Danusha covered Kasia's dirty, wrinkled hands with kisses.

Part Two

ADAM

✠ ✠ ✠

Chapter 10 / *May 1399*

Brother Vincenty's forehead creased in annoyance. "The Hebrews have a trick," he said, "which we should have tried with Marcin from the very beginning. When a Hebrew boy is taught to read, his teacher puts a drop of honey on the first letter. The boy touches the honey, then tastes his finger to discover that learning is sweet. Here is Marcin, thirteen years old, and he still stumbles through the words of the Pater Noster."

"Let Adam read for you," Danusha said, pushing him toward the scroll unrolled on the table. "Read for Brother Vincenty, Adam."

"You know I can read the Pater Noster, Mother," Adam said. "Let me try something different, so I can practice new words. Here at the bottom it says, *'Communicantes, et memoriam venerantes in primis gloriosae semper. . . .' "*

"Enough! I know that Adam can read well."

Adam raised his eyes from the scroll to glare at the monk. As usual, Brother Vincenty looked away from him. Brother Vincenty had never bothered to instruct Adam; all the skill he'd mastered came from sitting quietly at the table watching his younger brother struggle with the mysteries of the hand-copied scrolls. Now he was not even allowed to display that skill. He felt the bitterness rise in his throat.

"Marcin," the monk said, chiding the younger boy, "you know that it has been my hope to have you join me in the monastery when you are old enough. How will you ever become a monk if you cannot read the prayers? How will you be a copyist if you cannot form the letters?"

Marcin shrugged and smiled his gentle smile. "If I can't be a monk, I'll be a woodcutter, like the man who had this cottage before us. I like to carve wood."

"Adam can be a woodcutter," Brother Vincenty said shortly.

"I don't want to be a woodcutter. I cannot get a staunch enough grip on the axe." Scowling, Adam thrust his hands beneath Brother Vincenty's nose, forcing the monk to look at them. The scarring on his hands had drawn the skin so tight that he could never straighten his fingers completely or clench them into fists.

Danusha's touch was heavy on his shoulders; Adam knew that his mother was signaling him to remain silent, vexed at him for his rudeness toward the monk. "I think the lesson has lasted long enough for today," she said. "Why don't you tell us news of the outside world, Brother Vincenty?"

The monk seemed irritated as he rolled the scroll, but when Danusha placed a mug of ale and a plate of honey cakes before him, his expression softened. "Well," he said around a mouthful of cake, "everyone in the Polish nation is elated that Queen Jadwiga is going to have a child at last. King Jagiello especially is overjoyed, as you can imagine. He wants to decorate her chamber with brocades and jeweled tapestries for the birth of the heir, but Queen Jadwiga refuses. She insists that everything be stark and simple. The only rich gift she'll allow in the room is a silver cradle sent by Jagiello's brother."

"Our queen is very much like a saint," Danusha murmured. Adam saw her eyes warm with the memory of the girl she'd once seen in the gilded carriage.

"Many people believe that she *is* a saint," Brother Vincenty told them. "Paralytics touch her hand and they walk again.

82

And did you hear about the miracle she performed on Corpus Christi day? Did I tell you about that?"

Adam straightened, his interest caught. "Tell us," he said.

Brother Vincenty cleared his throat with a swallow of ale. "There was a procession along the River Vistula," he began. "The queen took part in it. While it was going on, a little boy—he was the son of a coppersmith—fell into the river and drowned. The people pulled him out and laid him on the bank, while his mother screamed with grief."

Danusha shook her head in sympathy, her face saddened for the unknown woman.

Brother Vincenty continued, "Queen Jadwiga heard the mother's screams and came to kneel beside her—you know what a tender heart our queen has. She took off her silk cape and spread it over the child's body while the mother still held his hand. Then"—the monk paused to build suspense in his listeners—"the boy's hand grew warm again. He came back to life."

Adam let out his breath as Danusha made the sign of the cross.

"A real miracle!" Danusha exclaimed, her voice husky with awe. "I remember the day I saw her, when she was just a child. Even then there was a special look about our queen. I wish I could see her again."

Adam's mind filled with thoughts of the queen whom his mother always spoke about with such reverence. Truly, she must be blessed by God, even though God had made her wait so long for this expected child. Brother Vincenty had told them that since the queen had conceived, the nation prospered as never before. The lakes were filled with fish, forests with game, and more twin lambs had been born in the spring than anyone could ever remember. Even their own garden seemed to flourish—after an unusually mild spring, the cabbages were twice as big as normal.

83

"Boys." Danusha's voice interrupted Adam's thoughts. "I just remembered that we need firewood. Go into the forest and cut some kindling. We have enough logs, but we need tinder."

Marcin jumped to his feet, glad of any excuse to take him away from Brother Vincenty's lessons, even though they were through for the day. "Come on, Adam," he said, touching Adam's shoulder as he passed. "I'll take the long axe. You bring the small axe."

"Wear your hat, Adam," Danusha told him.

"I don't need it. The trees will shade me," Adam answered.

"Adam, the sun's still high. You know what happens when you get too much sun. I don't want you to . . ."

Adam had stalked through the door, leaving his mother's words unfinished and leaving the hat inside on its peg. Marcin had to hurry to catch up to him.

"Whew," Marcin said, as they left the clearing. "I thought that reading lesson was never going to end. Why do I have to read anyhow? I'm good at carving wood. Why isn't Brother Vincenty satisfied with that?"

"Why should you complain?" Adam asked. "I'd like to be a scholar, but he won't even bother to teach me. And I want to be a monk, too, but no, it's always Marcin this and Marcin that. It's you he loves, ever since you were small enough to sit on his lap and pull his fat cheeks."

"I wish we could trade places," Marcin said.

"So do I." Adam glanced at his golden brother, at Marcin's fine-featured face and wide blue eyes. Marcin looked like the angels that decorated the illuminated scrolls Brother Vincenty brought to their cottage; he gave them the ones the copyists had spoiled. Their mother often said that Marcin not only looked like an angel, he had the disposition of one, while Adam sometimes fell into moods as black as the ink that had spilled on the ruined scrolls.

84

Marcin caught Adam's arm, saying, "Why don't you ask him if you can be a monk?"

"No, I'm not going to ask him. Let him ask me first."

"What if he won't? Are you just going to keep quiet and keep on getting madder all the time?"

Adam didn't answer. He didn't know the answer. He knew that because they were runaway serfs, they were safe only as long as they stayed in Krol Forest under the protection of the monks. He supposed he'd always be tied to the cottage in Krol Forest and to his mother who loved him but fretted over him too much. And if it ever did happen, if he ever got the chance to leave his home and his mother, Adam wasn't altogether certain whether he wanted to. He scowled. It was easier to feel irked than to know what to do about the things that irked him.

The way he looked—that upset him most. Though not a word was ever spoken aloud about his appearance, Adam knew that he was ugly. Each time Brother Vincenty came to the cottage, Adam watched the monk's eyes slip past his scarred, hairy face to focus on something to the side of him or over his head. And his mother—when the winter evenings were long and Adam stared into the fire as Danusha sat stitching their clothes or spinning wool—how often her glance rested on his face as she sighed deeply, not even aware that she sighed, her thoughts pressed so densely within her that the spindle fell unnoticed to her lap.

Only Marcin seemed unaffected by Adam's ugliness. Good-hearted, simple Marcin loved him with no reservation. And Adam loved Marcin back, but sometimes, on those long, confining winters' eves, he gazed at Marcin by the same flickering firelight and felt a stab of bitterness in his soul because his brother was so handsome.

Marcin had been striding along whistling to a song thrush, which fluttered from tree to tree whistling back. Lengthening

85

his strides, he turned to Adam and said, "Let's see which one of us can take the biggest steps."

"I don't feel like playing silly games," Adam growled. "But I'll do it anyway," he decided, "just to show you that I'm bigger and faster than you are."

Adam took the longest steps he could; Marcin nearly matched them. Though he was three years younger, Marcin was growing fast. Their mother said it would be as exciting as a horse race to see which of her sons finished his growth at a greater height, but Adam believed he'd be the taller. He already stood a handsbreadth taller than Danusha.

When Adam pulled ahead, Marcin started to run. Adam grabbed him and they scuffled, falling to the ground in a wrestling match. They rolled over and over, getting pine needles and bits of leaves on their clothes as they pummeled one another. Adam's blows became harder; the resentment he felt against Brother Vincenty made him set upon Marcin with a ferocity too harsh for roughhousing.

"Get off me!" Marcin yelled when Adam pinned him to the ground. "You're breaking my back!" Adam drew back at once, afraid that he'd really hurt his brother, but Marcin rolled away and sprang to his feet like a cat. "You didn't hurt me at all," he laughed. "I just said that so you'd let me up. For all your black moods, Adam, you're as soft-hearted as a new-hatched chick."

Adam swung one last cuff at Marcin's neck, then brushed dirt from his own clothes.

"We better get the wood chopped, " Marcin said, going back to pick up the axes they'd dropped along the path. He swung at a fallen oak a short distance from the footpath. "Look at me, Adam. I'm pretending that I'm hacking up Brother Vincenty's scrolls."

"I'll pretend I'm hacking up Brother Vincenty himself," Adam answered, as he began to chop the dead branches from a low pine. He clenched his fingers as tightly as he could around the axe handle. He'd wound a strip of rag around the smooth wood of the handle to give himself better purchase, but he was still unsure of his grip when he cut wood. "Marcin," he called, "if you could carve a new handle for this axe, a wider one, I think I could hold it better."

"Fine. I'll do it when we go home. I'm going to keep that old handle, though," Marcin said, "so I can make something out of it. See how smooth the wood is? If Brother Vincenty could bring me a drawing of Saint Catherine, I could carve a nice little statue of her to put on old Kasia's grave."

Adam remembered the old woman with fondness. "I think Mother misses Kasia," he said as he reached to chop a higher branch. "Mother says a woman needs another woman to talk . . . ow! I've cut myself." The axe blade had bounced off the limb, opening a gash in Adam's arm.

"Adam, you're bleeding bad!" Marcin threw down his axe and ran to his brother.

Adam's stomach turned as he stared at the bright red blood gushing from his forearm. Then he became aware of the pain.

"Ugh! That looks awful," Marcin said. "You better wrap something around that. I don't have a rag . . . wait a minute, I'll unwrap the rag from your axe handle." With fumbling fingers Marcin untied the long strip of cloth, then tightened it around Adam's bleeding arm. "It's no good. You better go home and have Mother bind it up right. You have enough bad scars on you already."

"I suppose you're right," Adam answered, as blood began to seep through the dirty rag. "Only I hope Mother won't make a fuss in front of Brother Vincenty. He thinks she coddles me too much already. I'll carry some of the kindling back with me." He was trying to act as though the cut was of little consequence, but his arm pained him.

"Forget the kindling," Marcin said. "Just get back to the cottage. I'll bring the wood when I come."

As he made his way back along the path, Adam thought

that it was fortunate they hadn't gone farther into the forest. He bent his elbow, squeezing his raised forearm against his upper arm, circling both with his other arm and pressing them against his chest. That seemed to slow the bleeding, although the cut still seeped.

He paused for a moment at the cottage door, which was slightly ajar, not wanting to burst inside and alarm his mother. His attention was on his wound—at first he didn't notice what Brother Vincenty was talking about. Then he heard his name spoken.

"Adam thinks I don't like him," the monk was saying, "but I do. It's just that I find it hard to look at him. The hair on his cheeks and forehead has grown so dark now, and his teeth . . . it's . . . its disconcerting to see teeth of a deep red color. I know this is a weakness on my part and I try to conquer it, but with no success."

Adam moved closer so that he could see through the narrow gap in the door. He knew it was wrong to give ear to other people's talk when they weren't aware of it, but they were speaking about him.

Brother Vincenty shook his head. "Adam has a fine mind; it pains me that he has to be kept here in seclusion because of the way he looks."

"Brother Vincenty . . ." Danusha leaned on the table to look across at the monk. "So often I blame myself for Adam's affliction. I think it's a punishment from God because I sinned with Reinmar."

The monk shook his head. "God is not so unjust as that, Danusha. Adam looks the way he does because his father looks that way."

"That's true, I suppose," Danusha answered, "though Reinmar always kept his face covered with the leather helmet."

"Perhaps if Adam would cover his face as Reinmar does," the monk began, "it might be possible for him to leave. . . ."

"No! He'll stay here with me. Aways!" Danusha's voice was vehement. "You were not there at Pan Lucas's manor the day the serfs stoned us. You didn't see the looks on their faces. If Adam left Krol Forest, people would set on him like dogs. On the manor they called him a devil-child, but now, with the dark hair on his face, you know what they would call him."

Adam squeezed his arm so tightly that blood stopped flowing from the wound; he felt as though his breath had stopped, too. He wanted to make his presence known so that the conversation inside would have to end, and yet he wanted to learn what it was that people would call him.

"Ah, the ancient belief in lycanthropy," the monk answered.

"Is that what it's called?"

"Yes." He looked at her sharply. "You don't believe such a thing about Adam, do you?"

"Of course not. As you say, Adam is like his father, and I now know Reinmar for what he was, a man with an affliction. But a man, nothing more sinister than that. He had no evil in him."

Brother Vincenty stared gloomily into his ale cup. "Yet when I think how that nobleman ill-used you, I am filled with disgust."

"Reinmar did not ill-use me!" Danusha spun around so that Adam could see the resentment in her eyes.

"How can you say that? He had bodily knowledge of you when you were an innocent girl of sixteen. He used you like a whore and gave you this ill-favored son!"

"Reinmar gave me an ill-favored son, but I loved Reinmar," Danusha shouted. "My wedded husband gave me a beautiful son, and I hated my husband."

"Hush, woman." Brother Vincenty raised his hand, bending his head as though listening. "I thought I heard some sound—other than your ranting."

89

Swiftly, Adam slipped around the stone chimney that jutted on the outside of the log wall, pressing himself into the farther corner so that he couldn't be seen from the door. He bit his lip to keep from moaning aloud again—the moan had escaped him before he was aware of it, whether from the pain in his arm or the scene he was witnessing, he didn't know.

He heard Brother Vincenty come to the door. "There's no one here," the monk said. "It must have been an animal or a bird that I heard." Evidently he left the door unclosed when he went back inside, because Adam could still overhear their voices.

He crept closer to the door, holding himself ready to bolt.

"If you have never told Adam who his real father is, perhaps you should do so," the monk said.

"No, Brother Vincenty, I'll never tell him. What good would it do? I have no idea where Reinmar is now, and both boys believe that Rydek was their father. Adam was only two when I married Rydek, so he has no recollection of the time before that."

"Perhaps you're right, my dear. Now I have to return to the monastery to be in time for evening office. The two-mile walk seems to grow farther as my belly grows bigger."

Adam drew back, then stole away with steps as soundless as he could make them, although he felt weighted down as if with heavy stones. He skirted the back of the cottage so that he would not have to pass the door. When he thought that he was safely out of hearing, he crashed through brush trying to forget what he'd just heard, but the words seemed locked inside his head; he remembered each phrase, each pause, each gesture. The word Brother Vincenty had used when he talked about what people would call Adam was one he hadn't understood, but the meaning of all else was as clear as if he'd known it all his life.

Marcin was handsome and perfect, while he was. . . . Since Danusha had given birth to both of them, the difference had to come from their fathers. Even though it was so many years before, he could remember Rydek, blond like Marcin, while Adam had brown eyes and hair that was black, both on his head and his face.

Panting, he ran along the creek bed until he came to a small clear pool where the water was still. He dropped beside it, bending over the smooth surface to see the reflection of his blemished, hairy face. The scars on his eyelids had hooded his eyes to make them narrow, animallike; his lips were drawn back in a grimace of anguish.

As he stared at himself, the scene he'd just witnessed began to fade, while cries that frightened him such a long time ago took their place, cries he'd begun to believe were only part of a horrible childhood nightmare. They came back to racket inside his skull.

"Devil slut! Slept with the Devil and begot the Devil's brat. Stand aside, Danusha, and let us see your devil-bastard make red water." All those voices, those angry faces . . .

Adam fell forward on both hands while the water, as if in answer to the taunts in his memory, slowly turned red with blood from his wound.

Chapter 11

"What's the matter with you, Adam?" Marcin sat back on his heels to study his brother. "You're tearing into that stump like you want to kill it. For the past week you've been really mean."

Adam leaned with all his strength against a pole he was using to pry loose the tree stump. He knew he couldn't move the stump until he dug more soil from around its roots, but the futile struggle gave vent to his turbulent feelings.

"Quit that, Adam," Marcin told him. "You're going to break open that cut on your arm. It's just starting to heal. If it bleeds again, it will scar worse and . . ."

Adam threw the pole on the ground to yell at Marcin, "And I'm already ugly enough from my scars, is that what you're going to say?"

"No, I wasn't going to say that." Marcin sat silent for a moment, hugging his knees as he watched Adam. "What's making you so mad?" he asked. "Did I do something?"

"No. You haven't done anything." Adam scowled. "Except to be good to look at and never worry about anything. And as if that's not enough, you're true-born."

"What does than mean—true-born?" Marcin looked puzzled.

"It means that you had a father. A father wedded to your mother."

"That's true. And so did you. We had the same father—Rydek."

"That's all you know." Adam picked up a stone and hurled it viciously at the tree stump.

"All right, Adam. You better explain. In easy words," Marcin added, "since I'm not as clever as you."

Adam slumped to the ground, rubbing his shoulder, which ached from the struggle with the tree stump. He wondered whether it would be fair to tell Marcin what he'd overheard the week before, yet he hadn't been fair to Marcin in acting so surly. And who else did he have to talk to? The secret burned inside him night and day, making him as sick as if he'd eaten spoiled fish. He couldn't sleep; he tossed at night because he heard those grating voices calling him a devil's bastard.

"You and I aren't real brothers," he said abruptly.

Marcin scoffed. "What are you talking about, Adam?"

"We're half-brothers. We have the same mother, but different fathers."

"Our father was Rydek."

"Your father was Rydek. Mine was named Reinmar. I heard Mother talking about it to Brother Vincenty last week. It was right after I cut my arm. You wondered why I took so long to get home that day—not till after you were already back. I told you it was because the loss of blood made me dizzy and I had to stop and rest, but that wasn't the truth. I went right home, but I didn't go in because I heard them talking together, about me. They said my father was Reinmar."

"Are you sure they said Reinmar?" Marcin asked. "Reinmar and Rydek—they sound a lot alike. Maybe you heard wrong."

"No, they said Reinmar. They said it often enough that I'm sure. He was a nobleman, and he mated with our mother and made her pregnant with me, but he didn't marry her. She loved him then, and she loves him still."

93

"Mother wouldn't do such a thing," Marcin said, his voice low. "She's a good woman."

"She did, though." Adam dropped his eyes, unwilling to see Marcin's troubled expression. "There was something more. This Reinmar always kept his face covered. Mother said he must have looked the same as I do."

Marcin was silent for a long time; Adam could tell that his words were making themselves felt. Marcin was slow to take in new ideas, but when he accepted them, he turned them over and over until the pieces fit. Finally he muttered, "You always worry too much about the way you look. Who ever sees you out here? We never go any place except to take wood to the monastery. Even then you keep your hood down over your face so no one can see you."

"Do you know why we have to stay out here?" Adam demanded.

"Because we're runaway serfs."

"That's what I thought, too, until I heard them talking. But that's not the real reason. It's because I look so horrible." Adam shouted to keep his voice from breaking. "That's not fair to you, Marcin. Why should you be kept here all your life just because of me?"

Marcin reached to clasp Adam around the neck, saying, "I don't mind, Adam. I swear I don't." Both boys had risen to their knees; Adam was almost pulled off balance by Marcin's clumsy embrace.

He began to cry. "Marcin, there are things I remember . . . terrible things. People screaming at me and at Mother. You were too little then to know . . . the world is awful! I almost forgot, till Mother's words brought it all back. But what will happen to me? I can't chop wood or carve like you do; all I can do is read, and what good is that out here? Some day Mother will grow old and die, like Kasia did. Then you'll hate me for keeping you here. I wish I could die right now!"

Adam felt his head seized roughly as Marcin pressed it

against his chest. "Don't talk like that. I'll never hate you."

Adam pulled away and wiped his face—the hair on his cheeks had grown wet with tears. "Marcin, don't ever say anything to Mother about what I told you. She doesn't want us to know about it, and I won't hurt her any more than I already have by being the way I am. Promise me."

"I promise."

Adam knew that once Marcin had given his word, nothing could pry the truth out of him. More than once Marcin had remained silent about something they'd done wrong, more to protect Adam than himself. Once when they were small and were playing with slingshots, Adam loosed a stone that killed their fine rooster. Danusha had been so vexed that she beat both boys with a switch. Although Marcin was only eight, he'd taken the beating without a whimper until Adam, filled with remorse, caught Danusha's arm and screamed that it was his fault. Marcin never would have told, even to spare his own hide.

Marcin got to his feet. "I'm going to wash in the creek now. You better come too, so we can milk the cow. The sun's going down soon. Before winter, I'm going to build a better shelter for that cow."

Adam looked at his brother in wonder. How could Marcin dismiss Adam's revelation from his mind so swiftly to worry about a cow? "Marcin, don't you care what I told you about my father?"

Marcin crossed his arms and frowned. After a moment, he answered, "It doesn't make any difference, does it? You're still my brother. What you said doesn't change that." He turned and walked away, gesturing for Adam to follow. "Come on, let's take care of the cow. I'm hungry. I want to finish work so we can eat."

Danusha was sewing a leather patch on a pair of Marcin's breeches when the boys went back to the cottage. "There's bread and curds for your supper," she told them, "also some spring greens I boiled. Eat them, they're healthful."

Marcin grimaced at Adam to show what he thought of boiled greens. They had just seated themselves on the long bench beside the table when they heard footsteps outside.

"Who could that be at this time?" Danusha asked, alarmed. "It's almost sunset."

Before she finished speaking, the door burst open. Brother Vincenty stood on the doorstep, panting, his face even rounder than usual because he was smiling so widely.

"I had to come and tell you this," he said, "even though it will be dark before I return. Such good news! Wait till you hear, Danusha!"

She jumped up and pulled him to the bench; he was speaking all the while. "A cup of ale for my thirst, there's a good woman. Now listen to this. Only last week you said that you wished you could see the queen again. You can, Danusha! She's coming to the monastery!"

Both boys rose to their feet as Danusha clasped her hands against her throat.

"A messenger came only this afternoon," Brother Vincenty continued. "It seems the queen will visit some monasteries and convents on a pilgimage to pray that her baby will be born healthy. Since we're only thirteen miles from Krakow, ours will be the third monastery on her route. From there she'll go to Wieliczka, then to one more convent before returning to Krakow."

"When?" Danusha asked, breathless.

"The day after tomorrow, sometime in the afternoon. You can come and wait in the courtyard with Marcin so you'll be able to see her."

"What about Adam?"

"I've already thought about that," the monk said. "Adam can stand in that thick copse of trees along the road just north of the monastery. There's a lot of shrubbery there, and he'll be able to look out and have a good view as she passes in her coach, but he won't be seen. The queen is going to be accompanied by a large retinue, but you'll know which woman is the queen, Adam, because her coach is gilded. It will be drawn by two white horses."

Now! Adam thought. Now I can confront them, to make them tell the truth. Make them explain why it's all right for Mother and Marcin to go to the monastery where they'll be seen by the queen's party, while I have to hide in the trees. I can force them to confess that it's my ugliness which keeps us prisoners here.

He was about to demand an admission of a truth he already knew, but his mother's elation stopped him. Danusha's words were coming in a rush of gladness as she told them for the hundredth time how she had seen Queen Jadwiga on her way to take the throne fourteen years earlier. "Of course, she'll look different now," Danusha chattered, "because she's a full-grown woman. Is it safe for her to be traveling in her seventh month of pregnancy? But then, I was working in Pan Lucas's kitchen only an hour before Adam was born."

I can't, Adam decided. I can't spoil it for her. He'd made Marcin promise never to tell the secret because it would hurt Danusha. How could he hurt her himself? He slumped on the bench, but no one noticed his silence because they were so caught up in anticipation over the queen's visit.

Brother Vincenty continued, bantering, "At least you could give me something to eat after I hurried all this way to give you the news, Danusha. I could have waited until tomorrow to come, but I thought you might want to prepare your clothing. Do you have something pretty to wear?"

Danusha set curds and bread before the monk as she answered, "I don't know whether I can still fit into my good green dress. It's been years since I tried it on. But if it's too

97

tight, the cloak will hide the snugness. Marcin's breeches are a disgrace, but I have some cloth, and I'll sew him a new pair tomorrow."

They sat around the table, discussing every detail of the queen's arrival as they ate. The heavy table was made of fine-grained oak, and in the winter before, Marcin had carved a pattern of leaves and flowers on its edges and on the sides of the bench. Danusha said there was nothing half so nicely decorated in all Pan Lucas's manor house. During the coming winter, Marcin planned to make a high-backed chair for their mother, carved with the same pattern.

After they had eaten, Danusha said to Marcin, "Take the lantern and walk along the path with Brother Vincenty. It's almost full dark now."

"And Marcin . . ." Adam put authority into his voice. "Stay the night at the monastery. There's no sense in your returning home while it's dark. Break your fast tomorrow with the brothers."

The others looked at Adam, surprised into silence.

He said, "Marcin ought to get away from this place once in a while. What reason is there for him to stay cooped up here always?"

Brother Vincenty cleared his throat. "It would please me to have you stay the night with us, Marcin," he said. "I've been anxious for an opportunity to show you a very old statue the abbot keeps in his room. They say it's more than two hundred years old and that it came from Italy. It's nicely carved."

"Then that's settled." Adam stood up. "I'll fill the horn lantern with oil. Get your cloak, Marcin. It will be chilly by the time you reach the monastery."

"Yes, master." Marcin grinned and made a mock bow.

Danusha said little after they were gone. She glanced at Adam more than once with questions in her eyes, but he disregarded her. He banked the fire in the hearth so that it

98

would last the night through, then took off his clothes and slipped under the sheepskin he used for a blanket. His pallet was on a wide, low shelf which had been built along the long wall of the cottage. Marcin's pallet was on the same shelf; they slept foot to foot, while Danusha used a mattress of rushes in the far corner.

"Good night, Adam," she called. "God be with you, my son."

"God be with you, Mother." He lay on his back with his hands beneath his head. He was wide awake, but for the first time in a week he was not plagued by the memory of those serfs who had attacked his mother long ago. His mind was filled instead with thoughts of Queen Jadwiga. He tried to imagine what she would look like, riding in the gilded coach; his mother had described the coach often enough that he could picture it. A queen would look different than common folk, but it had been so long since he'd seen any woman other than his mother and old Kasia that he could not conjure an image of one, queenly or otherwise. Yet Jadwiga was kind to common folk; Brother Vincenty had said she worked miracles . . .

Miracles!

He sat straight up in bed. Danusha, not yet asleep, called, "What it is, Adam?"

"Nothing, Mother."

"You're sitting up. I can see you in the light from the fire."

"It's . . . it's a flea, I think. Something bit me."

"A flea!" Danusha sat up too. "From that dirty old sheepskin! I don't know why you insist on.. . . "

"Go to sleep, Mother."

He could hear her sigh with vexation, then she was silent. Adam let his thoughts return, going over and over in his mind all he'd heard about the miracles. Paralytics walked, a dead child came to life. Surely that was the greatest miracle of all, to bring life where there had been death. Jesus himself

99

had done such a thing with Lazarus, and even the followers of Jesus considered that his greatest miracle. If the queen could make such a wondrous happening take place, surely she could make Adam whole again—take the hair and the scars from his face, make his teeth white like Marcin's.

He would have to plan carefully. How could he approach the queen to ask for a miracle?

Chapter 12

"Why are you so anxious to leave?" Marcin asked Danusha. "The sun's only been up for a little while."

"I'm too excited to wait here much longer. Besides, what if Queen Jadwiga should come earlier than she's expected? Then we would miss her arrival. Adam, I wish I'd had enough time to make you a new shirt. That one still has bloodstains on it from when you cut your arm."

"The queen won't see my shirt because I'll have my cloak . . . I mean, because I'll be standing back in the trees." Adam glanced sharply at his mother. He'd almost betrayed himself, but Danusha was too preoccupied to notice.

"I've wrapped some bread and cheese in this cloth for you, Adam. You may have a long wait beside the road, and you'll get hungry. Marcin and I will eat at the monastery. Does my dress seem too tight?"

"No, Mother, you look fine." And she did, Adam thought. Her hair was bound up in a coif of the whitest linen. The green gown—stored in the wooden chest for so long—was so different from the simply cut dresses of undyed wadmal cloth that Danusha always wore that his mother looked unfamilar and resplendent. Danusha said that the green had faded somewhat, but to Adam it seemed perfect, complimenting the bit of honey-colored hair which showed beneath her coif.

"Let's start out, then. I'm going to take my good cloak with

101

the fur trim. It will be too warm to wear, so I'll carry it while we walk, but I want to put it on when the queen comes. You don't have to take your cloak, Adam, since no one will see you."

"I might get cold while I'm waiting," he answered. "No sunlight can get through that thick growth in the copse." He would need the cloak so that he could cover his face with the hood when he spoke to the queen.

They shut the door behind them, then went into the forest to walk leisurely along the path. The boys grew impatient with their slow progress, but Danusha said she didn't want to hurry; if she exerted herself, perspiration might stain her good dress. "Do you know, once before when I wore this dress, on the day I first saw the queen, a mounted knight mistook me for a noblewoman."

"That'll happen again today, Mother," Marcin said, smiling. "When Queen Jadwiga sees you, she'll think you are a duchess. I'll be sure to stand far away from you, so the queen won't see that you have such a common-looking son."

"Marcin! Such foolishness!" She cuffed him playfully across the shoulder. Danusha was so high-spirited that she seemed almost as young as her sons, Adam thought. He wondered what his mother had been like at his age, then realized that when she was hardly any older, she'd gone off with Reinmar, his father. His face stiffened.

After they'd traveled three-quarters of the distance toward the monastery, Marcin said, "Here's the place you turn off, Adam. Go straight through these trees toward the road. You'll come out close to the copse."

"I'll find my way, don't worry," Adam replied. "I know these woods as well as you do."

"Adam." Danusha embraced him. "I wish you were going with us."

"I don't mind at all, Mother. God's truth, I don't." The excitement was growing so high in him that he couldn't wait to leave them, afraid they might read it in his face. "I'll see you in a while. God be with you."

"And with you."

At last he was free of them. He hurried through the trees. Twice his cloak caught on briars; he took time to loosen it carefully. It wouldn't do for the hood to be torn, he wanted it to shadow his face so the queen wouldn't be put off when she first saw him. Afterward . . .

Adam turned away from the direction that would lead to the copse, intending to wait farther up the road so that he could stop the queen long before she approached the monastery. When he reached the rim of the forest, he looked carefully along the roadway to be certain that it was deserted. No other cottages were anywhere near that part of Krol Forest, therefore no one else should be waiting along the wayside for the queen's cavalcade.

For quite some distance he walked along the edge of the road, enjoying the openness. Rain hadn't fallen for the week past, and the brown dust rose up to coat his worn shoes. He raised his face to the clear sky, savoring its warmth for a moment, then lowered his head to keep his skin from burning.

At last he decided he'd gone far enough, and he sat down beside the road to wait. The sun had not yet risen to the height of midday. It might be hours before the queen's party reached him.

As he waited, he imagined what would happen that day, picturing the scenes in his mind. When the queen's carriage approached, he would call out to her; she would signal to her courtiers to stop the procession. Adam saw himself kneeling in the dust with his face covered by his hood. In a strong voice, using the finest words he knew, he would beg for her help. "I need a miracle, Your Highness. Take away my ugliness and make me look as perfect as my brother."

Then the queen would reach out to touch him. Would he

feel anything happen to his body as the miracle took place? Made whole, like the leper in the Bible, he would follow the cavalcade to the monastery. First he'd go to the chapel to give thanks, as the good leper did, afterward he would search out his mother. She would not recognize him at once, but then, throwing her arms around him, she would weep with gladness. Later they could leave Krol Forest. Marcin would learn to be a sculptor, and Adam could attend the university at Krakow, where Brother Vincenty had told him the greatest teachers in Poland were gathered. After he learned all there was to learn, he'd come back to don the white robe of a Cistercian monk. He pictured himself as Brother Adam, with an unmarked face and smooth, strong hands.

The warm sun was making him sweat. He rubbed his forehead with the corner of his cloak. An ant crawled up his arm; he slapped it. It was past noon now. He decided to wait in the shade of the trees because he was growing too warm to sit with his hood pulled down, and he did not want new blisters to form on his face. Surely he'd have enough time to prepare himself before the cavalcade approached—it would make enough noise that he'd hear it far in the distance.

As time dragged on, doubt began to nag him. What if the queen wouldn't stop for him? No, he had to believe in her. She was his only hope. Remember, she had brought the dead child back to life. If she could do that, it would be a simple task for her to cure Adam.

To pass the time, he wove a garland of wild asters, a gift for Queen Jadwiga. He could present it to her after she healed him. He had begun a second garland for his mother when he heard the first faint sound of horses' hoofs.

Adam's hands shook so much that he had difficulty fastening the clasp of his cloak. Brushing bits of wild aster from the garment, he arranged the hood so that it covered most of his face. His heart beat hard in his throat; he had to breathe deeply to quiet it as he hurried to the road. Once there, he dropped to his knees.

He couldn't see! The hood came too far over his eyes. Folding it back to just above his eyebrows, he covered the rest of his face with his raised arm. He must be able to see well enough to look for the gilded carriage. When the queen stopped, he would lower the hood again.

The first group of horsemen came by at a slow walk. They glanced at Adam, but did not pay him any heed. No doubt they were used to beggars lining the queen's route and thought Adam was nothing strange.

A half dozen knights followed wearing tunics of bright colors, but Adam ignored them, peering into the distance to watch for the gilded coach. It was coming! The sun beat off its sides harshly enough to hurt his eyes.

"Queen Jadwiga!" he shouted again and again, even before she was close enough to hear. "Queen Jadwiga, please stop!" His voice was hoarse and his words were muffled by the arm which covered his mouth, but as the coach drew near, he cried her name until the queen turned her head toward him. Relief almost choked him when he saw that she raised her hand for the coachman to stop.

Quickly, Adam pulled the hood over his face, but not before he had taken in her appearance. She was tall, even when seated, richly dressed, with large dark eyes and skin which should have been olive-toned but looked sallow. She appeared tired and ill.

"Queen Jadwiga," he said again, stammering.

Her voice was soft and deep as she asked, "What is it you want? Do you need money?"

"No, Your Highness, I need a miracle."

His words sounded too loud in his own ears. Everyone must have heard them because the entourage grew silent except for the shuffling of the halted horses. Adam wished he

105

could see what was taking place, but he was afraid to uncover his face.

The queen sighed. "It is not true that I can work miracles," she said, sounding weary. "Yet I will help you in whatever way I can."

"Better be cautious, Your Majesty," a gruff voice spoke. "With his head covered like that, he might be hiding some vile disease. You wouldn't want to catch any sickness now."

To his horror, Adam saw the point of a sword slipping under the edge of his hood. As he felt the hood lifted upward, he yelled, *"Don't!"* But it was too late. The hood fell back to reveal his face.

He was so close to the queen that he could see the terror in her eyes when she recoiled from him. Her hands flew to her swollen belly as if to protect the child inside her. Then she seemed to crumple, falling across the seat of the coach.

"What has he done to the queen! God in heaven!" The horses reared into one another as the mounted knights tried to turn back toward the carriage, some of them leaping off their mounts to run to the queen.

Shouts rang out. "Grab him! Get that . . ."

Adam leapt to his feet and raced toward the forest, leaving the garland of wild asters behind in the dust. Briars and branches reached out to tangle his clothes, but he knew the forest, and his terror propelled him forward. Behind him he could hear the clatter of armor as knights swarmed after him, unable to move as fast as Adam because they were weighted down by their weapons. They cursed as they slashed at branches with their swords, their noise covering the sounds Adam made as he slipped through the trees. Escaping as silently as a fox, he worked his way farther and farther into the forest, breaking into a run when he thought it was no longer necessary to move quietly.

At last he threw himself to the ground, sobbing so hard he retched. Queen Jadwiga had fainted with fright at the sight of him! What would happen now? They would take the queen to the monastery, where his mother would hear what Adam had done. She would be humiliated, and Brother Vincenty would be furious.

For a long time he remained on the floor of the forest, pounding the dirt and groaning in his shame. It had been witless to think that the queen could cure him. Not even God could do anything with the likes of him! He was nearly grown, yet he'd acted like a callow child, thinking he could have a miracle just for the asking. He would have to go away. He could not face his mother or Marcin again. It seemed that half a day had passed before he pushed himself to his feet, determined to leave his home, if not forever, at least until he could come to terms with his disgrace.

Taking a roundabout route, he worked his way through the trees until he neared the clearing where the cottage stood. He moved carefully, uncertain whether there was a need for caution. The knights had probably given up looking for him, and Danusha and Marcin wouldn't have returned home yet; he would have time enough to go inside and take some food, the few clothes he owned, and the small axe. Then he would disappear deep into the forest and try to find some sort of shelter, perhaps an animal cave far enough away that Marcin couldn't find him, where he could live throughout the summer. When the weather turned cold, he'd come back home again. By then he hoped he could face his mother.

When he had almost reached the edge of the clearing so that he could see the cottage, he stopped short. Four armed knights waited next to the door.

Chapter 13

It was then that Adam first realized danger.

Until that moment he had been so consumed with remorse for his stupidity, so agonized over what his mother and Brother Vincenty would think of him, that he had not worried overmuch about the knights who chased him at first. They had followed him only a short distance into the forest, then given up the pursuit.

But seeing them beside the cottage, Adam knew fear. Late sunlight glinted on their round helmets, breastplates, and four drawn swords. Two of the knights talked together, the other two watched the entrance of the forest path. Adam did not dare move, although he was out of their sight in the thickness of the trees.

When shadows stretched into the clearing and covered it, Adam crept back into the thicket. He would have to lose himself in the dense growth during the night, then leave Krol Forest before the sun was high the next day. Although he knew the forest better than anyone except Marcin, he doubted that he could elude a large company of soldiers if they made a thorough search for him.

During the night he shook with cold, even though he had the cloak to wrap around him. He slept badly, starting up at every animal sound or bird call. As soon as the sky had grayed enough that he could separate the dark shadows of the trees, he started north, not knowing what lay to the north, but deciding that he could escape more quickly if he followed a single direction.

By midday the woods thinned and ended. Tilled fields spread out before Adam—people were working in the new crops. Beyond the fields stood a large stone house. Adam lay flat on his stomach, trying to find a passageway that would keep him out of sight of the working serfs. As he lay there, an armored horseman became visible in the distance, riding hard toward the fields. When the rider drew close he reined his horse; a few serfs came in answer to his call. The rider leaned over to talk to them. When they shook their heads, he rode on toward the stone house.

They're searching for me, Adam realized. Soldiers must be going out in every direction to ask whether anyone has seen me. Although it was only early afternoon, he would have to stay where he was until it grew dark enough that he could cross the open fields without being seen.

Returning to the heavier growth of the woodland, Adam passed the hours searching for food. Berries were useless—it was too early in the season for them, but he found mushrooms and dug the roots from a patch of spring violets. They only seemed to heighten his hunger.

When the sun had almost set, he returned to his vantage point overlooking the fields. The serfs were shouldering their hoes, walking slowly to a cluster of small huts which circled the stone house. Long after the last of them had entered their huts, Adam waited, until the first star shone in the darkening sky.

Crouching low, he ran, half stumbling, through the planted furrows. A full moon rose; if any persons had been about, they could have seen him in its bright light. The fields seemed endless. He reached a stream, startling a doe that had come to drink with her fawn, but Adam had a great need for water after his exhausting run through the fields, and he threw himself head down at the stream.

109

The moon was high overhead when he reached the safety of another woodland, and there he spent the night much the same as before. By the second day, again almost at midday, he had reached the edge of that stretch of forest, but instead of coming out into farmland, he saw rising in the distance the walled fortifications of a large town. Small farms dotted the clear area surrounding the town; one of them was only a few hundred feet away from Adam.

All through the afternoon he stayed just inside the shelter of the trees, watching the activity on the farm nearest him. A man and a woman hoed a small patch of garden next to a thatched hut. Chickens pecked in the dirt around a half-fallen chicken coop which stood some distance from the hut. Adam's hunger was making him desperate; what edible growth he'd been able to find in the forest had made his bowels flux. He needed food with some substance to it to give him strength to continue his escape. As the day wore on he remained hidden, memorizing every part of the small farm that he could see.

After dark, when the farmer and his wife disappeared indoors, Adam made his way toward the farm. So that it wouldn't hamper his movements, he left his cloak folded next to a high oak tree; he would return for it afterward. He stayed flat on the ground, crawling toward the chicken coop. If he could slip into it quickly enough and find one or two eggs before the cackle of the chickens aroused the farmer, he could run away before the man had a chance to see him in the moonlight.

When he was just a few feet away from the coop, the hens began to cluck. Adam stopped, holding himself so rigid that his muscles cramped. After a while, silence settled once again. Adam ran the last few feet to the coop, lifting first one hen and then another as he searched frantically for eggs. He couldn't find any, and the hens were making an ungodly din.

He heard the sound of pounding feet. Adam caught one of

the hens in his arms and ran outside, almost colliding with the startled farmer. "Chicken thief!" the man yelled, lashing out his fist to strike Adam hard in the stomach. Adam grunted with pain and dropped to his hands and knees, expecting to be struck again as the hen escaped with a noisy flapping of wings.

The blow did not come. Cowering, Adam raised his head.

The farmer had staggered backward, his face contorted with fear. "Go away!" he stammered. His arms were raised as if to ward off a menace. "Don't hurt me! Take my chickens— you can have all of them."

Adam tried to run, but the wind had been knocked out of him. He gasped for breath, falling forward on his hands again and again as he fled into the darkness. Behind him he heard barking—a young dog ran after him, nipping at his heels, playful and excited, not knowing whether Adam was a friend or a quarry.

"Gresha, come back!" the farmer shouted, but the puppy stayed beside Adam, darting around him in circles, almost tripping him. The farmer made no move to follow.

Adam went only a little farther before he fell to the ground, groaning, waiting for his breathing to become easier. The puppy rushed up to lick his face, then bounded away, yapping. Except for the dog's barking the night was silent in the bright moonlight.

When he felt that he could stand again, Adam looked back toward the farm. Far past it, he could see the light of a lantern swing beside a moving form, but instead of coming toward him, the light was moving away in the direction of the city walls.

The town was half-circled by a hill; Adam scrambled up its slope hoping the dog would grow discouraged and stay behind. But the animal persisted, leaping up easily after Adam.

Halfway up the slope Adam came upon a wide path which had been cut into the hill, rutted as though from the wheels of

111

many wagons. He followed the path, breathing hard from the climb and the soreness in his middle. He hadn't gone far when he noticed an opening in the wall of earth which rose to his left.

"A cave," he said aloud. At that moment it seemed God-sent. Adam entered it, groping in the blackness which surrounded him completely after he'd gone only a short way inside. The dog no longer followed him, but whimpered from the mouth of the cave.

Never had Adam experienced darkness so complete, but it promised him safety. With his hand against the rough dry wall, he moved slowly, placing one foot cautiously in front of another to feel for any sudden dropoff in the blackness.

The passage led deeper and deeper into a cavern. Instead of growing narrower, as he expected it would, the corridor seemed to widen the farther he went. When he kicked a stone, the sound of it echoed hollowly as though the cave's walls were a great distance away. For what must have been a quarter of a mile, he felt his way, descending a long tunnel, until at last he judged he would be safe.

Then he sat down, hugging his stomach because it still hurt him. The blackness was eerie—he could see nothing. The silence smothered him as much as the dark; it grew so heavy on him that he could hear blood coursing through the veins in his head. After a while he stretched on the floor of the cave and fell into a doze.

The sound of footsteps and the voices of men intruded into his dreams, making him cringe on the floor. Then he started up in fear, because the voices were real, not loud but racketing as they bounced off the walls.

"Are you sure he came into the salt mine, Captain?"

"We can't be sure. The farmer said his dog followed the werewolf, then Boydan found the dog sitting at the mine entrance. So he might be in here. Boydan and his men are

112

searching the eastern gallery—the rest of you stay close to me. Lift your torches higher."

Dazed, Adam sprang to his feet, scraping himself on the rough wall. Behind him he could see the pale orange glow of torchlight haloed by an uncanny shimmer. The torches looked farther away than the mens' voices sounded, but Adam realized that the voices were magnified by the vastness of the closed-in cavern. The men were still far enough away that their lights didn't fall upon him.

He crept deeper along the passageway, hampered because he couldn't see. The men were shortening the distance between themselves and Adam. Suddenly his groping fingers felt a crevice in the wall, wide enough that he could squeeze inside it. He pressed his body into the cleft and waited with terror as the footsteps echoed nearer and nearer.

The light grew brighter, illuminating walls of dark, glittering salt; the whole cavern was made of salt—floor, walls, and roof.

"Careful, men. Stay close together."

"Do you think it's the same werewolf that frightened the queen, Captain?"

"No doubt. Unless there's a pack of them running loose. Fan out a bit now. This gallery is widening. We're getting almost to the statuary chamber."

"God's blood, Captain, I don't think I want to find him in here. He might leap out and tear our throats."

"Don't fuss at the captain, Jaroslav. There's six of us, all told. If the werewolf gets you, the rest of us will avenge you."

"Shut your mouth, Simon. That's not funny."

The walls' crystalline reflection was growing so bright that Adam could see huge black shadows cast in the forms of moving men.

"How far should we go, Captain? These salt galleries go on for miles."

113

"All the way to the end, if need be. What do you think you're paid for, Mikolaj? If you didn't want to do soldiers' work, you should have been a milkmaid."

"Soldiers' work is fighting, not poking around salt mines for a werewolf," Mikolaj grumbled.

"How do we know the creature is a werewolf?"

"The farmer said he had hair all over his face and red teeth that dripped with blood in the moonlight. He was eating a live chicken."

"Werewolves don't eat chickens. They eat people."

"Will you shut up, Simon?"

"All of you stay alert, now. We've reached the statuary chamber. Search around each of these carved pillars to make certain he's not behind one of them."

At that moment a young soldier came up beside the crevice where Adam was hiding. Adam held his breath, willing the youth to pass by without seeing him, but the soldier stopped and swung his torch in an arc to peer all around him. At the end of his turn he stared directly into Adam's face.

"He . . . he . . . here . . ." The boyish soldier tried to sound the alarm, but his voice wouldn't work. His torch shook so much that the flame danced crazily while his other hand groped for his sword hilt.

Adam leaped at him, knocking the torch to the floor. As the soldier shrieked Adam lunged around him into the immense grotto.

"There he is! Right there! Go after him!"

Adam raced across the high-vaulted chamber. Statues of angels and saints had been carved into pillars of salt left to shore up the ceiling, their faces glittering blankly out of the dark salt, their robes falling in stiff, sparkling folds. Adam became confused in the dazzling light, unsure which of the forms were statues and which were real men.

"Easy, fellows. We've got him now. He can't get away."

The six men circled Adam, holding torches in one hand and

114

drawn swords in the other. Their torches were thrust forward like weapons, reflecting orange and gold brilliance off the salt crystals as though the sun had broken into infinite tiny jewels.

As the circle of soldiers tightened around him, Adam whirled, searching for a space to break through. In the unearthly light he saw a statue of an angel carved from the dark salt, its raised wings unfolded. He backed against it for protection as the soldiers closed in.

His body and hair were seized roughly; he was jerked forward.

"Hold your light over here. Let's have a look at him. God, what is he? He's not a wolf or a man either."

"Tie his hands and feet," the captain ordered. "Don't let him get away. Half the countryside has been trying to find him."

"If we tie his hands and feet, Captain, he might change into a wolf and slip the bonds. Better we put a rope around his neck."

Adam felt a band tighten against his throat. It choked him; he tried to cry out, but could only gasp.

"Loosen that rope! You're going to kill him before we get him to the surface. We want to keep him alive."

"What are we going to do with him, Captain?"

"I'll take him to Krakow," the captain answered. "I told you to tie his hands and feet—now do it! Two of you pick him up and carry him to the outside."

Tightly trussed, Adam was picked up by two soldiers. His body sagged so that his back scraped against the rough salt of the mine floor, and he arched upward.

"What is he trying to do? Watch it, he might be changing into a wolf!"

"He's no wolf, Jaroslav, you idiot," the captain barked.

"But the farmer said he dropped down on all fours and ran like an animal."

115

"The farmer's an idiot, too. Didn't you see the prisoner's face in the torchlight? He's just a lad—hairy and ugly beyond belief, but no wolf."

"Well, anyway, I wouldn't want to ride with him all the way from Wieliczka to Krakow," the soldier muttered. "Not under a full moon. Who knows what might happen?"

"Then you can come with me, Jaroslav."

"No, Captain!"

"Just to see that nothing evil will happen on the way. For a soldier, you're as cowardly as a rabbit."

They reached the mouth of the mine in much less time than it had taken Adam to descend it. He hadn't realized how cold he'd been in the cavern until the warmer outside air blanketed him. Still he shivered, so numb with despair that it seemed nothing worse could happen to him. He hardly listened to the men's talk.

"One of you go to the east gallery and tell Boydan to call off the search. Where are the horses?"

"Down there a little way. They're ready and waiting. Shall all of us ride to Krakow with you, Captain?"

"No, just Jaroslav. Untie the prisoner's feet and put him on Simon's horse. Then run a rope under the horse's belly and tie it around the ankles of this wolfman, or whatever he is. That way he can't jump off."

When the soldiers lifted Adam into the saddle, he crumpled and would have fallen if the captain hadn't caught him.

"Sit up there! Here, tie his hands to the pommel. Hold onto it, boy. You've got an eight-mile ride ahead of you. What's the matter, haven't you ever ridden before?" The captain's voice was gruff, but he seemed more curious than hostile.

Adam turned to look at the man. He was large and heavy-muscled, wearing a breastplate molded to the shape of his broad chest. His face was seamed, more from weathering than from age.

"No. Never," Adam answered low.

116

"Then hold hard on that pommel. That'll make it easier for you. I don't want you sliding all the way around and landing with your head against a rock and your feet on top of the saddle. I'll lead your horse behind mine. Jaroslav, you ride at the rear."

"Good luck, Captain," one of the soldiers called in the darkness as the horses began to move. "Hope you make it all the way to Krakow."

"Save your worry. I don't need it."

Weak, sore, and hungry, with his hands tied to the pommel and his feet tied beneath him, Adam slid from side to side as the horse walked. He wondered dully what would happen to him when they reached Krakow, but it didn't matter any longer.

When the road widened, the captain reined back to ride alongside Adam. "How did you come to look so awful, boy?" he asked.

Adam dropped his head, not knowing what to answer.

"Do you live around these parts? Who's your father?"

"I have no father."

"Any mother?"

Adam was silent.

"It's eight miles to Krakow, and we've traveled only one of them," the captain said. "It will ease the journey for both of us if we talk along the way. You'll find that I'm a much more pleasant fellow than the head warden at the Krakow jail. If you don't answer my questions, I won't box your ears or bang your head against the wall or twist your elbow behind your back till it touches your neck. He'll do all those things, and worse."

Adam's hands tightened on the pommel.

"You didn't really mean to harm the queen, did you?"

"No."

"Why did you stop her coach?"

It all seemed so long ago that Adam had to search his mind

117

to remember why he had wanted to talk to Queen Jadwiga. "To ask for a miracle," he said after a while.

"What? What did you say?"

"A miracle."

The captain stared. "I can guess what you wanted to ask for." He took off his helmet to wipe sweat from his forehead, then turned his eyes on Adam again. "They say you cast a spell over the queen. She's been sick ever since you stopped her on the road."

"I can't cast a spell," Adam said wearily. "Any more than the queen can make a miracle."

"No, I don't suppose you can. I'm sorry to have to turn you over to the warden in Krakow, because I think you're just a poor, miserable, innocent, ugly lad. But I have no choice." The captain spurred his horse, leaving Adam to follow in the dust. The hoofbeats of Jaroslav's horse grew softer as the young soldier in the rear left a widening space between himself and Adam.

Chapter 14

"Captain Pavel, good to see you again. Good God, what's that you've brought with you?" The one-armed jailer looked aghast as he caught sight of Adam.

"Just a wretched, worn-out lad, Janus. Listen, I don't want this boy put in a cell with any of your cutthroat prisoners. Keep him away from the bad ones—they'd tear him to pieces. Do you have an empty cell where you can stow him?"

The jailer answered without taking his eyes from Adam. "Maybe, Captain. I could put him into that little room down by the end of the hall, though it's not much more than a closet. Where'd he come from? Who is he?"

"He's the so-called werewolf who frightened the queen near the Cistercian monastery. See that he gets something to eat, will you? He's half-starved, he told me. Here's money to pay for his food."

Captain Pavel threw a coin into the air, and the jailer caught it, grinning. "See, Captain? I do as good with one hand as most fellows do with two. I'll try to look after this wolf-boy for you, but I can't say what will happen when Warden Klemens finds out he's here. You know how that Klemens is."

"I know, Janus. Do your best. I'll stop by when I'm in Krakow the next time."

"Yes, sir. Good night, Captain Pavel. Or more likely I

119

should say good morning. It's nearly dawn." The jailer approached Adam, who was leaning against the doorway. "Come along, prisoner. Do you have a name?"

Adam tried to think whether he should tell his name— would it harm his mother and brother? His mind was too clouded to reason. "It's Adam," he mumbled.

"All right then, Adam," the jailer said, "Don't try to run or nothing. No, I guess you lack the strength to run even if you wanted to."

Adam's arm was gripped tightly above the elbow as the jailer led him down the hall, stopping before a heavy door. "This building is a jail now, but it used to be the house of one of those lords from the Sejm Parliament. Kept his idiot son locked up in this little room so no one would see him. It's where I'm going to put you. Not much space inside, but you'll be safe from the rough fellows in the big cell. I'll bring you something to eat as soon as I can. Captain Pavel must of took a like for you to give me half a grocz for your food."

Adam stumbled and fell as Janus pushed him into the high-walled cubicle. He lay where he fell and slept at once, waking only for a moment when Janus deposited some bread and a jug of water inside the door. He slept through most of the day, getting up only long enough to eat the bread and drink the water from the jug. Then, because there was no other container in the cell, he urinated in the empty jug and slept again.

"So this is the werewolf?"

Adam rubbed his eyes to look up at a slightly built young man standing over him. Janus hovered behind the man, just inside the doorway. "This is Warden Klemens," the jailer told Adam, gesturing with his single hand that Adam must rise from the floor. When he climbed to his feet, Adam stood taller than Warden Klemens.

"It was you who cast a spell on the queen," the warden stated, scanning Adam's face with cold gray eyes.

120

"I didn't cast a spell on her. I only stopped her to ask for a . . . a favor."

"The queen has been ill since you stopped her."

"That wasn't my fault. . . ."

"Silence!" Warden Klemens' fist slammed against Adam's ear, making his head ring. "Speak only in answer to my questions, and address me as 'sir'." He smoothed his narrow mustache, then asked almost in a whisper, "Have you made a pact with the Devil?"

"No, sir."

"Come now, do not be afraid to tell me the truth. I'm genuinely curious. Did you make a pact with the Devil?"

"No, sir."

"Then how did you learn to turn yourself into a wolf, and how did you learn to cast spells?"

Adam rubbed his burning ear, wondering the best way to answer so that he wouldn't be hit again. "I don't know how to cast spells, sir, and I can't turn myself into a wolf. I look this way because . . . I've always looked like this."

"No Christian man looks like you, nor any pagan either," Klemens said, his voice still soft. "Only demons are covered with hair, you know. And look at your teeth—all red, the color of Satan. Perhaps you have a tail, too, like a demon. Show me whether you have a tail." When Adam hesitated, Klemens barked, "Strip off your clothes and show me your tail."

Adam fumbled with his shirt, pulling it over his head.

"Your breeches, too. Take off your breeches and your shoes so that we can see whether you have cloven hoofs. Now turn around. Hmmmm, how strange. Look at him, Janus. His body looks like that of any other youth—no tail, no cloven hoofs. He's hairy only on his face. Perhaps he's part demon, part wolf, and part man. I wonder which part is which. Can you tell, Janus?"

Adam shivered in his nakedness, feeling more frightened

121

of this small man than he'd been of all the soldiers together.

"What was it, boy?" Klemens asked. "Did your mother mate with a wolf or a demon? Or perhaps with both of them, on alternate nights." He laughed in a high snigger, then scowled. "Put on your clothes. You disgust me. Ah, look at that, Janus. There are bloodstains on his shirt from when he ate the live chicken."

"No, those stains are from. . . ."

Klemens hit him again. "I said that you were to speak only in answer to my questions."

As Adam pulled on his breeches, the warden's eyes darted around the small room, stopping at the earthenware jug. "What is this, Janus? You've brought wine to the prisoner?"

Janus looked puzzled. "No, sir, I didn't bring him wine. Only water."

"And he's changed the water into wine?" Klemens' voice rose in a crescendo.

"No!" Adam began to tremble. "When I woke up, I had to pass water and there was no place else to do it, so I used the empty jug. Every time I pass water, it's always that color."

Klemens' eyebrows raised until they touched the edge of his velvet cap. "You see, Janus, he is certainly in league with the Devil. There is our evidence." He pointed to the jug. "Christ turned water into wine in his first miracle. This demon mocks Christ by turning water into wine through his vile body. This is very dangerous. Cross yourself, Janus. We're surely dealing with a devil, are we not?"

"That's not true." Adam backed against the wall. His legs felt so marrowless that he feared he would fall. "I'm not a devil."

"Where do you come from, devil-wolf?" When Adam didn't answer, Klemens asked, "Do you live near Wieliczka? Answer me!" He sprang forward to seize Adam's throat.

Adam choked, barely able to answer, "Krol Forest."

"Ah. Krol Forest. Where you put the spell on the queen." Klemens released Adam, then pulled a square of silk from inside his embroidered sleeve. Carefully he wiped each finger of the hand that had held Adam's throat. "We'll learn more about this. I will send an investigator to Krol Forest. Keep the prisoner locked up, Janus. Even a wolf cannot escape if the door is securely barred. But see that he doesn't cast a spell on you. And have a care that he doesn't bite you with those red teeth." Klemens turned and left the cell, followed by Janus.

Adam sank to the floor, shaking, but only a moment later he heard the scrape of the bolt which barred the door. Janus came into the cell again, a bucket in his hand and a cheese under his arm. "Here's a slop pail for you, and something to eat." He set them down, then picked up the earthenware jug to stare into it. "God's nose, boy, maybe you *are* in league with the Devil. I never saw such a thing as this before in my whole life. I don't know which of them to believe—Captain Pavel, or Warden Klemens. I fought all over the country when I was a soldier with two good arms, but I never saw a man make red water out of his own body."

Janus set down the jug and scratched his tousled hair, staring at Adam. "You're a puzzlement and a wonder, boy. But I guess I'll go along with what Captain Pavel says, because I never had no cause to doubt him before. It was under Captain Pavel that I was fighting when I lost my arm, and it was him that staunched the bleeding with a red hot sword blade to save my life." He raised the scarred stump to show Adam. "So I'll do what Captain Pavel says and treat you right. Only, Warden Klemens won't like it if I treat you too good, so we won't let him know."

After Janus left, Adam began to worry seriously about what might happen to him. He'd felt so much menace coming from Klemens—the man seemed to breathe evil. Adam searched

123

the cell to see if there might be a means of escape from it. The room was so narrow that he could pace no more than four steps in any direction, and it was altogether bare—nothing but walls of flat gray stone surrounding a floor of the same gray stone. High on one of the walls a narrow slit of window let in whatever light shone into the room, and some sounds from the street outside—voices of people and the clop of horses' hoofs. Adam looked for handholds with which he could pull himself to the window and look out, but the gray stones of the wall had been fitted so smoothly that there was not a single crack wide enough for his fingers to fit into.

As he examined the window, trying to think of a way to reach it, he heard a trumpet. It played a long tune, then broke off before the melody came to an end.

Once again Janus came into the cell, this time carrying a stool. "Here's something to keep you off the floor," he said.

Adam asked him about the strange trumpet sound.

"Oh, that," Janus answered. "That's just our city trumpeter playing to announce the time. He stands on the high tower of Saint Mary's Church and blows his little tune every hour. The song breaks off like that because more than a hundred years ago, a trumpeter was killed by a Tartar arrow on that very same note. You'll get used to it. After a while you'll not even notice the trumpet. I hardly do."

As soon as Janus left, Adam stood on the stool to try to reach the window, but the opening was still far above his fingertips. He leaped, but even from the stool he couldn't jump high enough.

For the next two days Adam sat on the stool, with nothing to do but think. Janus came in two or three times each day, always chattering a long while, but when he left, Adam counted the hours by listening for the trumpeter's song. Often he heard noise from the street, voices raised in laughter or in argument, but he had trouble making out the words. He

124

passed the tedious hours by worrying about his mother, who would not know what had become of him, and about what Klemens would do to him when he came back. The warden had not returned since the first visit. Adam asked Janus if anything had been decided about him, but Janus had heard nothing.

On the third day he woke to the clamor of bells, heavy bells which sent vibrations through the stone floor, middle-sized bells that sounded like the one from the Cistercian monastery, small bells clanging rapidly with high tones. Soon people's voices were added to the clamor of the bells, people shouting, laughing, singing, cheering. Adam wanted to ask Janus what was happening, but the jailer did not arrive the way he usually did. Instead, late in the morning Captain Pavel entered the cell.

"Great news, Adam!" he cried. "Queen Jadwiga has had her child. It's only a girl, but that's no misfortune. As people say in the village where I grew up, a girl this year, a boy the next."

Adam stood up. "The queen—is she still sick?"

"I don't truly know, but I'd guess she has recovered. A mother is always so happy with her firstborn that she soon forgets she ever felt poorly. And a queen's just like any other woman when it comes to that. She's going to name the princess Elizabeth Bonifacia, Elizabeth for Jadwiga's mother and Bonifacia for the pope. Now I have other news for you, Adam. I've been to see your mother and your brother Marcin."

Adam's heart lurched with both hope and concern. He had refused to tell anyone his mother's name because he wanted to protect her from trouble with the soldiers, yet he longed to hear whether she was in good stead.

"Don't look so worried, lad. I only went to help them. I heard that Klemens was sending a spy to Krol Forest, so I

125

rode over and got there ahead of him. I told the monks not to tell anyone where your home is." Pavel's lips widened in a grim smile. "I despise Klemens so much that it gave me pleasure to thwart him."

"What about my mother?" Adam asked. "You said you saw her."

"I'm coming to that. I walked through the forest to your mother's cottage and told her all about what happened to you. The poor woman was crazy with worry. The minute I told her where you were, she was ready to fly out the door to come here. I had a hard time stopping her."

"Why shouldn't my mother come?"

"It would be the worst thing she could do. Klemens would be on her like a cur tearing at a rabbit. Anyway, I promised your mother that I'd try to get you released straightway. It should be easy, Adam. Now that the princess is born, there's no reason to keep you locked up."

A frown crossed Pavel's face. "At least, I think it should be easy. First I must talk to that worm Klemens about it. Tomorrow is the princess's christening day, the perfect time to ask for your release. It's an old custom that certain prisoners are set loose when a royal birth is celebrated."

"Is Warden Klemens the one who will decide if I'm set free?" Adam asked, feeling less hopeful.

"Don't fret yourself about him. Leave him to me. I'll go talk to him now, if I can find him."

All through the afternoon, as Adam waited, the bells never let up in their pealing, proclaiming the news that Poland had a princess. Adam's head began to ache from the clangor and from his anxiety in wanting to hear from Pavel. But at nightfall when Pavel came back into the cell, the man seemed annoyed.

"Klemens won't let you go," he announced bluntly. "He says he has proof that you're a demon in league with the

126

Devil—something about your passing red urine. Is that true?"

"Yes."

"Why didn't you tell me what happened, Adam, instead of letting me go in there like a damned fool to demand your release? Klemens just laughed in my face. Well, nothing can be done now except to petition the queen, and that will take some time, considering the uproar Krakow is in over the birth of the princess. I'll do my best, but it would have been better if you'd told me about that water to wine blather that Klemens is using against you."

He left the cell abruptly, allowing the heavy door to stand open behind him. When Janus hurried to close it, Pavel called back, "Don't be so qualmish, Janus. Where could he go even if he got out?"

By the next day the noise and clamor were even louder as noblemen by the hundreds rode to the cathedral for the christening. Janus explained it all to Adam. Trumpets blared almost continuously to announce the dignitaries, and at nightfall the scent of wood smoke filled Adam's cell. "The people've lit bonfires in honor of the new princess," Janus reported. "Everyone's out there dancing and singing and getting drunk, and I'm going to do the same as soon as I can. I've brought you some wine so you can celebrate too, Adam. Pretty soon, maybe, I'll be able to let you out of here, and you can go home to your mother. Captain Pavel tells me she's a beauty."

"She is?" Adam looked up in surprise. "Pavel said that?"

Janus grinned. "Do you want to hear what Pavel said—all of it? He said she has eyes like the sky in summer, skin like roses, and breasts like ripe melons. His very words, I swear to you." Janus laughed out loud, shaking his head. "To hear the leathery captain talk like that—I could hardly believe these ears sticking out from my head."

127

Adam stared at Janus, only half trusting his words. Could Pavel really have looked at his mother that way? As a woman? It was a disturbing idea, one Adam did not want to think about.

On the following day, the bells ceased abruptly and the streets were silent. Janus was downcast when he brought Adam's food. "It's all over," he said gloomily. "The baby died. Princess Elizabeth Bonifacia is dead."

Chapter 15

Klemens began with the same question he asked each time he had interrogated Adam since the death of Princess Elizabeth Bonifacia. "Where did you learn to cast spells? Answer me, Adam. Was it your mother who taught you, or was it the Devil himself?"

"No one taught me, sir," Adam replied wearily, sitting on the short stool with his arms around his knees. At the first session Adam had stood, but in a brusque voice the warden had told him to sit. Klemens preferred to look down on his victim.

"If no one taught you, then you learned by yourself. When you made your pact with the Devil, you suddenly discovered that you had the power to cast spells, is that correct?"

"No. I made no pact with the Devil, and I can't cast spells."

Klemens half closed his eyes and began a new attack, one he hadn't used before. "I have learned that a witch lived in your hut when you were a child," he said. "Undoubtedly it was the witch Katarzyna who introduced you to the black arts."

"Katarzyna? You mean Kasia! She was no witch. Kasia was just an old woman who lived with us."

"Ah, yes. She had an unnatural fondness for you, I have been told. You were very young, and you had no other friends except the old witch. Naturally she told you her magic secrets." The cell was stifling in the July heat; Klemens took out the square of silk to touch it against his forehead.

"Kasia didn't know any magic. She was only an old woman. Sir."

"An old woman. How old? A hundred years? Two hundred, three hundred years? How old was she?"

Adam pictured Kasia's wrinkled face; she'd looked ancient from the time he first remembered her. "She said she didn't know how old she was."

"Ah . . . she was ageless," Klemens murmured. "She was a true demon not bound by time as we know it. She had probably been in existence since Lucifer took the bad angels into Hell."

Adam tried to keep his voice steady. Whenever he hesitated or became confused, Klemens goaded him without mercy. "Kasia was just a serf," Adam answered. "She wasn't a demon."

Klemens changed his tactics again. "What was your father's name?" he asked.

"Rydek," Adam replied, looking down.

Klemens laughed lightly, sniffing his perfumed piece of silk. "Each time I ask you that question, Adam, you quiver. You always say Rydek, but you quiver, and you drop your eyes." The warden moved his index finger, with its long, pointed nail, slowly before Adam's face. "If you would tell me the truth, confess everything to me, I might be persuaded to spare your life. If you don't tell me the truth, then I will burn you. Now I will ask you once more. Who was your father?"

Adam watched Klemens' finger as it snaked before his face. He was shaken that Klemens had learned about Kasia, yet one of the monks could have mentioned that innocently enough without revealing Danusha's whereabouts. But what else did Klemens know? Why was he asking about Adam's father? How could he have learned about Reinmar?

130

"My father's name was Rydek," Adam answered. "He is dead."

"I am a patient man, my dear werewolf," Klemens said curtly, "but my patience is not infinite. Soon you will admit to me that your father's name is Satan, though he is sometimes called Lucifer or Beelzebub."

Adam almost smiled with relief, but managed to keep his face impassive. So *that* was what Klemens had been gnawing at! He wanted Adam to say that his father was the Devil.

"If it were only up to me, Wolf," Klemens went on, "I would have your mother thrown into jail alongside you, and I would have the two of you burned together in one raging bonfire. However, your mother has found a protector, my sources tell me, in that low, vulgar Captain Pavel. I suspect she pays for his protection with her ripe body."

"Don't talk about my mother!" Adam leaped off the stool to lunge at Klemens, but the warden tripped him. When Adam fell hard, Klemens dropped on top of him, his knee pushed against Adam's neck. Adam tried to fight, but the pressure on his neck stunned him; he could barely hear Klemen's voice over the roaring in his ears.

"You mustn't press your luck, Satan," the warden hissed. "You're alive at this moment only because the queen has forbidden any executions during the period of mourning for her infant. Even though"—he drove his knee harder into Adam's neck—"I have repeatedly sent word to the palace that the werewolf . . . responsible for the princess's death . . . languishes here in my prison."

Klemens got to his feet, leaving Adam spread out on the stone floor. "You waste too much of my time," Klemens fumed. "I will find a more effective way to deal with you." When he left the cell, he instructed Janus to have a second bar installed on the door.

At midday on the seventeenth of July Adam was startled by

the booming of the deepest bell in Krakow. It tolled so slowly that Adam found himself holding his breath between each peal, wondering if the next would come. He listened for the sound of voices on the street, but there were no shouts of joy or excitement, only an unnatural silence, which was broken moments later by the sound of a woman wailing. The bell continued to pound for more than an hour. Adam covered his ears with his arms and pressed his head against the wall, waiting for Janus to appear.

When the jailer finally came, Adam could see that he had been weeping; his good arm was raised to wipe the tears from his cheeks. "Queen Jadwiga is gone," he said hoarsely. "She died. Today at noon."

Adam felt his throat knot. Immediately the queen's image filled his mind, as she had looked the day he stopped her coach: the sallow complexion, the shadowed eyes filling with terror when she saw him, the way she'd clutched at the child inside her before she lost consciousness. "Do the people think that I . . . caused her death?" he stammered.

"No, Adam. The people have forgotten about you. Only Warden Klemens keeps blaming you, but that's just so he can look big in the eyes of the lords in the Sejm Parliament. He wants to be made a lord himself and be called Pan Klemens. Pan Klemens—ugh! The sound of it sours the mouth like vomit." Janus spat on the floor. "Now that the queen's dead, I suspect that Klemens'll say that you cast a spell on her to make her die. But anyone should know that if you could cast spells, you'd of cast one on Klemens long ago."

Adam nodded. "I hate him. I hate him so much that . . . What will he do to me now?"

"God alone knows. He'd burn you if he could, but there won't be no executions till after the queen's buried."

Adam felt the hair rise on his neck. "When will that be?"

"Not for weeks. The great lords and ladies from all over Europe need time to travel to Krakow for the burial services."

"Won't the queen's body . . ."

"Rot, you mean, from the heat?" Janus finished for him. "She's supposed to be a saint, remember? Saints don't stink when they're dead like us ordinary folks do. Besides, the coffin will be closed day after tomorrow."

"If she was a saint, why didn't she save herself?" Adam asked, his voice low and harsh.

"Don't say such things, boy. If Klemens hears you talk like that, he'll use it against you, and you're in enough trouble already. The queen died, if you ask me, because she didn't want to live. Lost every one she ever loved, poor woman. First that prince fellow from Austria. After that her mother was murdered, her sister died, and finally her baby. She just got tired of losing everyone, I suppose." The jailer's eyes filled with tears again. "There'll never be another one like our Queen Jadwiga."

All day as the death knell tolled, Adam sat hunched against the wall. Guilt seeped into him a drop at a time, like rain water dripping through thatch on a roof. If he hadn't frightened the queen, would she have had the child so early? Janus had said the birth was premature and hard; in spite of her tall stature, the queen was too narrow through the hips. But if the baby had been born later, as it was supposed to be, perhaps it would have been strong enough to survive. If the child had lived, Queen Jadwiga would still be alive. Adam put his head on his knees, too despondent to cry. He had spoiled so many lives.

It would have been better if he had been the one to die at birth instead of the innocent princess. It would have been better, Adam felt with certainty, if his mother had never conceived him by Reinmar, that father who was supposed to be like Adam, the man who had vanished, leaving Danusha burdened with a son who caused nothing but grief. Adam had ruined not only Danusha's happiness, but now that of the whole Polish nation.

The next day Janus let himself into Adam's cell, his face distressed. "Oh, God, boy, the worst is happening, and I don't know how to stop it. Klemens is having a cage built. He's going to put it in the street in front of the prison and put you into it. 'Let the people see the werewolf who killed their queen,' he told me. He's going to whip up the crowds to anger against you, and there's nothing I can say to keep him from it. I'll send a message to Captain Pavel in Wieliczka, but I don't even know if he's there or someplace else now."

Adam hunched farther into his corner. It's what I deserve, he thought—a fitting punishment for all the misery I've caused.

"If Queen Jadwiga was alive, she'd soon put a stop to this madness," Janus went on, nervously rubbing the stump of his mutilated arm. "The queen never allowed no torture of prisoners or public pillory. But the queen's dead, and the king's locked himself up in Wawel Castle half-crazy with grief, they say, so no one can get near him. I'll send a message to Captain Pavel right away. If we can find him, he'll do something, you can bet."

Janus hurried out of the cell, then hurried back in. "Heed me, Adam, when it's time for you to go to the cage, let me take you and don't fight none. If you try to hold back, Klemens'll have you trussed up like a pig. Do whatever he says to make it easy for yourself."

The next day they led him down the hallway, Klemens and Janus and a husky, slow-talking jailer named Viktor, out into the summer sunlight. After so many weeks inside Adam couldn't see at first in the bright light, then he made out the form of the wooden cage standing in the street. It had been crudely built of thin poles crossed in a grid and tied together with leather thongs. Three feet wide, five feet long, and four feet high, the whole shaky structure was elevated on legs to stand at shoulder height above the ground. Janus and Viktor boosted Adam through the open end of the cage, then lashed

134

a door of poles over the opening. The rough poles dug into him, but when he shifted from a sitting position to his knees it was no less hurtful, and the cage was too short to allow him to stand.

Klemens watched from the side, his lips twitching in a half-smile as Adam crouched inside the cage. "I want a guard to stand here at all times," he said, "to make certain that the werewolf does not get out of this stockade."

"I'll do it, Warden. I'll stand guard," Janus volunteered, but Klemens sneered at him.

"Do you think I'm a fool?" he asked. "This werewolf already has you under his spell, Janus. If I leave you out here with him for hours at a time, he might demonize you altogether. I consider myself responsible for your immortal soul, Janus. No, not you. Viktor can stand guard." He gestured to the other jailer. "Viktor, see that the prisoner is put into his cage at nine every morning and kept there until the Angelus rings in the evening. Then lock him into the cell inside. He changes into a wolf each night at sunset, you know."

Viktor turned his unblinking eyes on Klemens. "As you say, Warden," he mumbled.

Klemens noticed a family of burghers approaching on the far side of the street. "Come here, citizens," he called to them. "Come this way. Look inside the cage. Here is the werewolf who murdered your queen."

As the burghers, a stout mother and father and four equally stout children, walked cautiously toward the cage to stare, Adam raised his arm to cover his face.

"Put down your arm," Klemens barked. "You are on display here, and the citizens want to see you. Open your mouth so they can see your red teeth as well as your hairy face. Viktor, if he tries to cover himself, prick him with your spear."

Adam closed his eyes as he bared his face, waiting for the

screams of horror, but they did not come. The woman sighed, "The poor queen—it was God's will," and the family nodded and walked away.

Klemens was furious. "What avails these people? And where is everyone? The streets are empty."

"They are at home saying prayers and mourning the queen," Viktor said in his impassive voice, "or else they are in the churches."

Klemens turned on his heel and walked back into the prison, making Janus go with him.

"The warden doesn't understand," Viktor muttered when they had gone. "The people are too sad to be angry." He shuffled his feet on the cobblestones, then leaned on his spear to wait for the hours to pass.

Adam looked around him. The street was narrow, with buildings two or three stories high joining each other in continuous rows on either side. It was midmorning, and the shadow of the eastern row of buildings covered him as he moved around trying to find a comfortable way to sit, but he found none. His body began to ache with the confinement and with the pressing of the poles against his flesh.

As the sun moved higher in the heavens, its rays beat down on him. The heat burned his skin and made him itch. He rubbed his face, knowing as he did that blisters were forming. He covered his face with his hands until the sun reached the western half of the sky, when afternoon shadows slipped over the cage.

During the entire afternoon only a few people passed by. When they stopped to stare at Adam, they wore expressions of awe, alarm, repugnance, or even pity. Each time Adam held himself rigid, expecting cries of horror, but the citizens of the large city of Krakow—where deformed beggars huddled around every church door—were used to grotesqueries.

After a second day spent under the midday sun, and a third

136

and a fourth, Adam's blisters broke into gaping red sores oozing liquid which crusted on the hair of his forehead and cheeks. Larger crowds began to collect, staring at him with curiosity and revulsion. The grief that had numbed the Krakovians at the death of their queen was beginning to subside. More and more people from the countryside poured into the capital to wait for the queen's funeral, and the heat and crowding made them irritable and excited. The country folk did not often get to see curiosities like Adam; they thronged the street.

Two or three times a day, Klemens mingled with the onlookers, telling them, "This is the werewolf who cast a spell over the queen, causing her death."

A few people could be counted on to cry out, "Burn him! Burn the werewolf. Revenge the queen!"

It was then that Adam began to feel the hatred reaching out from them. When he raised his arms to cover his face—if Klemens was not around, Viktor never stopped him—big boys would run up to the cage, shaking it violently, and then laugh as Adam clutched the bars to keep from falling.

Fear stayed with him so constantly that it never left, even after he was returned to his cell in the evenings. His dreams were filled with contorted, leering faces and arms that stretched to pluck and tear at him, while voices howled in his head until he woke up sobbing. When he was led back to his cage in the mornings, he wanted to fight and shriek. Only Janus's firm grip on his arm and Janus's low voice encouraging him, warning him that he must be submissive, kept him from bolting into the arms of the mob.

Yet Janus had been forced to tell Adam the disappointing news that Captain Pavel could not be reached. He had been sent to Hungary to escort the dead queen's brother-in-law to Krakow for the burial ceremonies.

On the hot afternoon of the last day of July, a rabble surged around the cage, laughing as a small boy on his father's shoulders prodded Adam with a stick thrust through the bars.

Adam wanted to cry out, but he'd learned that every time he opened his mouth the crowd was aroused more than ever by the color of his teeth. These were not Krakovians; they were country people who found it amusing to harass Adam the way they would a trapped animal. They jostled Viktor in their attempt to get close to the cage, and he cursed them under his breath.

When a perspiring, red-faced woman planted herself in front of Viktor, he growled, "What do you want?"

"Do you think he's truly a wolfman?" the woman asked.

"I think," Viktor answered deliberately, "that he may be a leper."

The woman's eyes widened. She backed away to where the street was less crowded, then picked up her skirts to run. "Leper!" she yelled. "Get out of my way! He's a leper!"

The people around the cage fell silent. They looked fearfully at one another, then drifted off until the street was deserted.

Viktor grinned at Adam and dropped his eyelid in a slow wink. "That'll keep them away for a while," he said. "Wish I'd thought of it sooner."

Chapter 16

So many people crowded Krakow to wait for the queen's funeral that it was impossible to ride a horse across Market Square. One of the Polish lords caught in the throng had to shout at those on foot to clear a path so that his horse wouldn't trample them; even so it took him a quarter-hour to get out of the square. Once he reached a side street, he jumped down to quiet his nervous palfrey.

The lord was on his way to Wawel Castle at the top of the hill, but because he was in no great hurry, he decided to take a more circuitous route through the less traveled streets. He wiped the perspiration from his face, smiling wryly as he felt his smooth chin—his wife had persuaded him to shave his beard, saying that otherwise he would look like a country bumpkin in Krakow. Since King Jagiello was clean-shaven, most of the courtiers followed his example.

A landowner from the Poznan district, the man was not familiar with the side streets of Krakow, but he knew in which direction he would find Wawel Castle. He remounted and headed that way. The crowds were less heavy than in Market Square; when he entered one of the smaller streets, he found it almost empty.

In the center of the street was a cage constructed of wooden poles, with a man, or youth, inside it. As he rode nearer the lord grimaced because the youth looked diseased. He peered more closely, then guided his horse all the way up to the cage.

139

For a long time he sat staring at the youth, at the matted black hair lining the cheeks and forehead, the oozing sores, the old scars. A thick-set guard leaned on his spear beside the cage.

The lord swung out of his saddle and walked to the guard. "Who is that person?" he asked, pointing to the cage.

"Just a prisoner," the guard replied, not bothering with the usual courtesy observed by a commoner speaking to a nobleman.

"Where does he come from?"

"Somewhere south of here."

"Do you know anything about his family?"

The guard frowned. "If you want to find out about him, go ask Janus. He's inside the building. You can tell which one is Janus because he only has one arm."

"Hold my horse." The lord handed his reins to the guard as he looked for the entrance to the building, which had a large carved door as though it belonged to a person of wealth.

Inside, the lord looked around him, sniffing the unpleasant odor usually found in jails or hospitals. Since no one seemed to be about, he banged his scabbard against the stone floor.

After a moment a stubble-bearded man came toward him, a man whose one shirt sleeve hung empty. "Are you Janus?" the lord asked.

"That's me. What do you want me for?"

"I want to ask about that prisoner in the cage," the lord replied.

The jailer looked suspicious. "What do you want to know about him?"

"What's his name? Who is his father?"

Janus narrowed his eyes. "Are you asking for yourself or for Warden Klemens?"

The lord was growing impatient. He ran a hand through his dark blond hair and frowned. "I don't know any Warden Klemens; I only want some information about that prisoner.

140

If you can't give it to me, direct me to someone who can."

"Well, sir"—the jailer's words came with irritating slowness—"maybe if you was to tell me who you are and why you want to know, I might give you an answer. That prisoner out there is a decent lad, and he's got enough trouble already without someone from the Sejm coming to bother him."

"I don't want to bother him," the lord said angrily. "Listen, I don't know that it's any of your business, but I was squire under a knight who had that same kind of affliction. I'm Pan Marek from Poznan. I know nothing of this Warden Klemens, but I would like to learn why that boy is being held captive, and who he is. Here . . ." He dug a coin from inside his tunic and held it toward Janus. "Maybe this will loosen your tongue."

"Pan Marek, you say?" Janus tilted his head, ignoring the coin. "I don't know as I've heard that name before. Do you come here often to sit in the Sejm?"

"Sometimes, when it's in session, but mostly I stay in Poznan. Why are you asking me these questions?" Marek demanded. "I told you why I want to know about the boy. Now answer me before I knock you down for your insolence."

"All right. It's just . . . poor Adam . . ."

"Is that his name? Adam? Where does he come from?"

"Near Krol Forest, where the Cistercian monastery is."

Pan Marek blinked rapidly. "Do you, by chance, know his mother's name? I assure you I mean no harm to the boy or his family."

"I suppose it won't hurt none to tell you his mother's name," Janus said, still wary. "It's Danusha."

Pan Marek took a deep breath and let it out slowly. "Have you ever seen this woman? Can you tell me what she looks like?"

"No, I never saw her, but I know what she looks like— someone mentioned it to me. She's blond and blue-eyed, a big woman with bre . . . well, never mind about that."

Marek could feel the blood pounding in his temples. "One more thing—do you know how old that boy is? His exact age. Here, I'll give you another coin."

"I don't want your money." Janus waved it away with his good arm. "Keep the money. I'll tell you anyway. Adam turned sixteen last month."

Marek leaned against the wall, counting in his mind. Growing excited, he asked, "Do you know whether this Danusha and Adam once belonged to a lord named Pan Lucas?"

"Yes, they did." Janus eyed Marek with surprise. "Adam told me once that some serfs stoned him, someplace on a manor that a Pan Lucas owned. Who are you?" he asked. "You come in here asking about Adam, but you already know plenty about him. Are you a spy for the crown?"

"No," Marek answered. "I've already told you that I'm . . . it doesn't matter. Why is Adam a prisoner?"

"He stopped Queen Jadwiga on her way to the monastery. The queen took a fainting fit at the sight of Adam, so he ran away. He was caught in Wieliczka by Captain Pavel, and he's been locked up here ever since. Warden Klemens is making him a scapegoat on account of the queen took sick after she saw Adam, and Klemens says that Adam cast a spell over her to make her die. He wants to burn Adam as a werewolf."

"Good God! Is there any chance that that might happen— that the boy could be executed?"

"Who's to say? Warden Klemens would do anything to get himself noticed by the lords of the Sejm. Adam's only hope is Captain Pavel, but he's not even in Poland right now, at least not that I know of."

Agitated, Marek drummed his fingers against his sword hilt. "That boy's no more werewolf than I am," he said. "He's only . . ."

142

"You know it, and I know it, and Pavel knows it," Janus interrupted. "Even Klemens knows it, damn his soul and bones, but it don't make a bit of difference to him. He wants Adam burned."

"I'll petition the king!"

Some of the wariness had gone out of the jailer's face. "No one can get to the king," Janus said. "Since Queen Jadwiga died, Jagiello won't talk to no one. He stays locked up in his chambers."

"There's bound to be some way to reach him," Marek declared.

"I don't know why you're interested in Adam, Pan Marek, but I'll tell you one thing—he needs all the help he can get. Each day he sits there under that burning sun, and he's getting sick from it. I don't know how much longer his skin can take it before he starts to fester and dies of poison in the blood. If you can help Adam, you better do it quick."

Marek could see that the jailer's concern was real. "Can I count on you to help, Janus?" he asked.

"I'd do anything I could to help that lad. Often I've thought of letting him go, but Klemens would string me up. And Adam couldn't escape nowhere anyway, looking the way he does. And besides, he's too weak."

"I won't ask you to do anything that will put you into danger, at least not openly," Marek told him, "but I'll need someone here to help me."

"There's not just me, but Viktor, too," Janus said, "that guard outside. Viktor hates what Klemens is doing to Adam. Both of us would help if you could get Adam out of here." Janus scratched his nose. "You know, sir, it's just come to my mind, I could be putting my neck in a noose, and Viktor's too, for what I'm saying to you."

"You can trust me," Marek said. "For four years I served as squire under a knight who . . . who looked the same as

143

Adam. It wasn't until the third year that I saw his face, when he was taken with a fever and nearly died. I had to care for him. I loved that man, and still do. He was like a father . . ." Marek choked on the word. If what he suspected was true, and the things he'd heard proved that it had to be, Reinmar *was* a father. To Adam. "I'll come back later, after I've had a chance to plan," he told Janus.

When Marek went outside, Viktor was standing in the same place, still holding the horse's reins. He looked at the lord with distrust.

"Have no fear," Marek told him softly. "I'm a friend. Janus will tell you."

Walking slowly, the way he would approach a frightened horse, Marek went to stand before the cage. When he reached through the bars, Adam drew back, but he gently touched Adam's hand and held it. "I knew your mother a long time ago," he said quietly. "I'm going to get you out of here. Just now I don't know how to do it, but you must believe that I will, Adam. Have courage."

The boy didn't answer. Marek could feel the hand trembling in his own. Adam looked ravaged; the lids were so swollen and scabbed above his eyes that the color of his eyes was barely visible. Marek unfastened his cloak and threw it over the top of the cage, saying, "This will shield you from the sun, Adam."

"Klemens . . ." Adam began, his voice guttural. "He'll take the cloak away."

"It's of no matter. Let it shade you till he does."

"Thank you," Adam whispered.

Marek was filled with such distress at the sight of Adam's suffering that he had to turn away. He took the reins from Viktor, handing the guard several coins. "Buy Adam something nourishing to eat," he said. "Even if he doesn't want to eat, force him. He needs his strength built up."

144

Viktor looked from the coins in his hand into Marek's face. "I'll do what you say," he answered. "Sir, if you want to help Adam, get him out of here fast. He no longer cares whether he lives."

In the evening of the next day Marek ate in the great hall at Wawel Castle. He'd spent the entire day trying to see the king; the room where he'd waited was filled with half a hundred other petitioners, some of whom had been waiting for more than a week, they told him. Jagiello refused to talk to anyone—not his brothers, the dukes, or the castellan, or the emissary from the pope. He raked himself with blame because he'd been away from Krakow on the day Jadwiga died, not realizing how ill she was.

Although the great dining hall was filled with noblemen, it was quiet, lacking the usual merriment of large gatherings. Sorrow over the queen's death had had time to diminish, but none of the lords wanted to lose favor with their grieving king by having it reported that they'd acted with levity during the period of mourning.

Marek sat at the long table next to a Krakovian lord who was wolfing his food. "Do you know anything about a Warden Klemens?" Marek asked the man.

"That upstart!" the lord snorted. He threw down his knife to wipe his mouth with his sleeve. "Born a niggling toady and he'll always be a niggling toady, no matter how much he schemes to rise into the Sejm. He's a rotten bastard, that Klemens. He'd hang his own mother if it got him any advantage. Why do you want to know about him?"

"No reason. I just heard the name, although he wasn't spoken of very highly."

"Huh! Little wonder. Everyone hates him, but he's smart and he's sneaky, I'll give him that."

"Does he have any real power?" Marek asked.

"Only with the lower level of bureaucrats like himself. No one of rank takes Klemens seriously. I only know the man because he arrested one of my stewards. For theft, would you believe it? As if I didn't know my steward steals from me. How else is a steward supposed to make a living? I went down to that jail and roared at Klemens—you should have seen him cringe. Vulgar little bootlicker!"

After he'd finished eating, Marek strolled, pretending idleness, through the halls of the castle, looking for the chamber where state business was conducted. A guard directed him to the right room, and Marek went inside. All the tables in the room were covered with mounds of paper in great disorder. The government was suffering from Jagiello's neglect.

Marek went up to the only person in the room, an official clerk who sat writing at one of the tables.

"I'm Pan Marek from Poznan," he said. "Recently I bought a large tract of forest—it needs to be marked down in the landholding record for the Poznan district. Can you get it for me?"

The official looked up in despair. "I'm working here by myself, sir. It would probably take me hours to find that record. Maybe days. No one bothers with anything around here since Queen Jadwiga died. Could you come back another time?"

"No, I'll be leaving Krakow tomorrow. I need the record now."

The man sighed and got to his feet. "Yes, Pan . . . Marek, did you say? I'll look for it, but I cannot promise that I'll find it."

As the clerk began to move piles of papers, Marek wandered around the room, stopping before a gold casque embossed with scenes from the life of Saint Stanislaus. "Does this chest hold the Great Seal of Poland?" he asked.

"Yes, Pan Marek."

"Could you open it to let me see the seal?" Marek asked. "I have never seen it. We lords from the country don't come to Krakow all that often. I'd like to have a look at it so I can tell my wife."

The clerk looked exasperated, but he came over to where Marek stood. "As it happens, I do have the key," he said, "although normally the castellan carries it with him. But the way things are around here since the queen died . . ." He pulled out a bronze key that was hanging on a chain hidden under the neck of his tunic. Marek heard a loud click as the door to the chest was unlocked.

"So that's it? Big thing, isn't it, almost as big as my hand. All gold, and there's the Polish eagle on it. The Great Seal of Poland, think of that." Marek turned to smile at the official. "Now I can tell my wife . . . what's that over there on the table?"

The clerk turned around.

"I think that's the tax record I want. Doesn't it say 'Poznan'? On that table over there—right on the edge."

As the man craned his neck to see, Marek slipped a bit of wax from his tunic. He'd carried it next to his chest for an hour so that it would soften. He pressed the wax against the Great Seal with such force that the muscles knotted in his arm, then removed his hand as the official turned back to him.

"No, it does not say Poznan," the clerk said, looking even more irritated. "That's not even a tax record."

Marek grinned sheepishly and scratched his head. "I never was very good at reading," he apologized. "Devil take it, man, if you haven't found that record by now, don't trouble yourself further. I'll take care of it the next time I come to Krakow."

"But you said . . ."

"Yes, but I can see you're busy. It can wait. Oh, one more

thing. I need a piece of paper to write to my wife. I can write better than I can read." Marek smiled as though he were a little drunk or a little foolish.

The official muttered as he locked the casque, then went to find a piece of paper for Marek. He was back at his table immersed in his writing, too busy to notice the change in the lord's expression as Marek strode out of the room.

When he reached an empty hall, Marek looked at the wax still in his hand. It was not a clear imprint; he'd made it too quickly and the wax had not been as soft as it should have been. But it looked official enough to deceive a niggling bureaucrat.

Chapter 17

The following morning rain pelted through the bars of the cage, soaking Adam thoroughly in only minutes. A half-formed thought brushed his mind—that rain would keep away the painful sun—but he had so much trouble holding onto thoughts that it soon lost significance. He lay doubled over in the cage, too feeble to move.

Viktor stood stoically beside him, now and then reaching up to wipe the rain from his helmet. Then the guard went inside the prison to return a moment later with the nobleman's cloak. He spread it across the top of the cage. "This will protect you a bit," he said. "I have kept the cloak hidden so Warden Klemens wouldn't take it."

Adam felt himself slipping again into darkness, the same darkness which came on him so often now, when he was no longer aware of anything but pain. Somewhere in the core of blackness his head began to throb with a sound—was it the rain which dripped on him through the wet cloak? The sound was harsher than rain; it was of horse's hoofs on cobblestones.

"Viktor," a voice said softly. "Where is Warden Klemens?"

"He's inside, Pan Marek."

"Can you find Janus without disturbing the warden? Ask Janus to come out here."

Sounds of footsteps; Adam had sunk too far into the dark to wonder about them. More voices, then the cage moved.

Adam opened his eyes as far as he could. The lids were so swollen that it cost him more effort than it seemed worth.

Viktor was unfastening the end of the cage. Janus and the nobleman stood beside Viktor. Who was the nobleman? Someone he'd seen once, something about his mother.

"Lift him carefully. Let me help you."

He felt himself pulled from the cage. He was confused; surely the whole day hadn't passed already.

"Tell Warden Klemens that you didn't learn my name," the man was saying to Viktor and Janus. "I have a forged document which you will give to him. It has an official seal, so he can't blame you for releasing the prisoner to me. After Adam is safe, I'll send someone to make certain that neither of you is in any trouble. If Klemens tries to punish you, I'll see that you're exonerated."

"Exon . . .? What's that mean, Pan Marek?" Janus asked.

"Let off without blame. I have friends who would use their influence for me if it became necessary. But I don't think Klemens will suspect that the document isn't real, so there should be no danger for you. Lift Adam onto my horse. God! He looks half-dead!"

"Here, take your cloak to wrap him with," Viktor said. "It's wet, but at least it will cover him."

"Adam!" Marek was shaking him. "Adam, listen to me. You have to help yourself. Sit up on this horse. I know you're sick, but you must gather all the strength you have."

Adam tried to remain upright in the saddle, but he fell forward against the horse's neck.

"He's too weak," Janus said.

"Never mind," Marek said. "I'll hold onto him while we ride. I'd planned to get a second horse just outside Krakow, but Adam is in no condition to ride. My horse is strong enough to carry both of us." Adam felt the horse shift as Marek mounted behind him; strong arms circled to support him.

150

The sound of running footsteps. "What's this! What are you doing?" Warden Klemens was beside them, his hands above his head to protect his velvet cap from the rain. "Who are you? Where do you think you're taking my prisoner?"

"I have written orders from the king," Pan Marek declared. "This prisoner is to be taken to a cell inside Wawel Castle." Marek held Adam firmly with one arm as he leaned to wave a paper before Klemens' eyes.

"Why didn't you come and tell me about it? What do you mean by riding off with my prisoner without informing me?"

"Does the king discuss his every decision with you?" Marek asked heatedly. "Now get out of my way. I don't enjoy dawdling here in a cloudburst."

Klemens grabbed the reins, jerking the horse's head. "You're not going anywhere until you prove to me that you come from the king. Let me see that order again."

"Read it fast, you pompous little ass!" Marek yelled so loudly that Adam cringed. "There's the king's signature, there's the official seal. Now let go of my horse or I'll report to the king that you do not obey his direct orders."

Klemens stepped backward, the anger draining from his blanched face. "No, my lord . . . no! Please don't do that," he stammered. "On the contrary, I would hope that you tell King Jagiello . . . tell him, please, that Warden Klemens has kept the prisoner confined safely all this time, merely awaiting the king's disposal of the matter."

"That's better." Marek snatched back the paper and put it inside his tunic.

"But, shouldn't we tie the prisoner so he cannot escape?"

"Escape!" Marek thundered. "He can hardly sit up in the saddle! If he dies before we're able to interrogate him properly, you'll pay for it, I promise you." Marek spurred his horse, leaving Klemens wringing his hands in the downpour.

"Hold on now, Adam, as best you can," Marek said into his ear as they turned the corner. "We have to move fast."

151

The throngs of funeral mourners who crowded Krakow were barely visible in the heavy rain. Those who had nowhere to stay pressed themselves against the walls of buildings or huddled in doorways for protection, leaving the streets almost deserted. Marek supported Adam as the horse crossed the city and trotted through the Wesola Gate; the palfrey did not slow until they had passed the cluster of huts ringing the city walls.

"That's the first obstacle out of the way," Marek muttered. "We're out of the city."

Adam leaned back against Marek's chest. "Where . . . are you taking me?" he asked.

"As far away from Krakow as we can get. We exited by the Wesola Gate so that if anyone saw us they will think we're on the road to Sandomierz. Now we're going to circle back through the woods until we reach the Poznan road. We have to put as much distance as possible between ourselves and Krakow. By tonight the worst danger will be over, and you'll be safe."

The growth of trees was thick; Marek pushed aside branches so that the horse could pick its way through the pathless forest. After a short while he halted the palfrey. "I have a rope, Adam," he said. "I'm going to tie you to me so that I don't have to keep holding you. I know how weak you are, but we have many miles to go before we get to the inn I want to reach by nightfall. Then we'll put you into bed, and you can rest for as long as you want."

While he spoke, Marek wound a rope around the two of them so that Adam was supported upright against him. The horse began to move again; after a little while Adam lost consciousness.

He came to his senses to find himself on the ground; his hands were being rubbed hard by Pan Marek. Adam moaned and tried to pull away.

"Thank God!" Marek said. "For a while there I thought you might . . . Listen, Adam, we're very near the inn. I have to wrap some strips of cloth around your face to look like bandages. When we reach the inn just stay silent—I'll do all the talking. Don't worry about anything."

The rain had stopped. Pan Marek lifted Adam to the horse, then mounted behind him as before. For another quarter mile they rode along a narrow highway which had turned to mire; the horse's hoofs made sucking sounds in the mud. Adam found it hard to breathe through the bandages on his face; he was beginning to drift into blackness again when Marek said, "This is the inn. Steady now—we're almost safe."

"Here, lad!" Marek called to a stableboy who ran to meet them. "Go tell your master we want a good lodging. After that, see that the horse is properly dried and fed."

Marek lifted Adam in his arms to carry him inside the building. When the innkeeper came toward them, Marek said brusquely, "Show me to a room—quickly. My brother is very sick."

"Uh . . . is it anything catching?" the man asked.

"No. He's a student at the university, and he got drunk and fell into a fire. His face is badly burned. I'm trying to take him home to our mother, but he's too weak to travel farther. We may have to stay here as long as a week until he grows strong enough to ride again."

"Yes, my lord," the innkeeper answered. "We've been filled up most every day with all the travelers going to Krakow for the queen's burial, but most of them are already there, so we do have a room empty."

"Good. Take us to it now, and fetch a candle. Then bring some soup for my brother."

Adam could hear the innkeeper's tread creak ahead of them as Marek carried him up a flight of stairs. "Careful, sir," the man said. "The steps are narrow. Your brother got drunk, you say, and fell into a fire? Poor fellow. These young lords don't know how to handle their wine, do they? Here's the room, sir. Not too spacious, but comfortable enough. Shall I light the fire? It's already laid. The air's turned a bit cool after the rain."

"Never mind, I'll light it myself from the candle." Marek placed Adam on the bed, saying "Now bring the soup, innkeeper, and something heartier for me to eat."

When the door had closed, Marek whispered, "I'm going to take the wet clothes off you, Adam, and the bandages, too. You stay under the blanket. Keep it over your face until our host has brought the food."

Adam could not help crying out as the wet shirt was pulled over his head. Marek wrapped him tightly in the blanket, then sat beside him on the edge of the bed. "Try to stay awake until you've eaten something," he said softly. "No one will search for us here; we can stay as long as we need to."

For the better part of four days Adam slept, waking only when Marek spooned soup through his blistered lips. Sometimes he screamed in his sleep, but Marek was always beside him, pushing him back against the bed when he rose up, laying cold cloths on his swollen eyelids. Once Adam smelled a pungent odor and asked dazedly what it was.

"Spearmint leaves," Marek told him. "The innkeeper's wife brought some for me to put on your face. I don't know about these things, but she said it would help burns, so I guess it might help your soreness too."

"It feels good," Adam murmured.

"Then I'll ask for more of them," Marek said, but before he finished speaking Adam was asleep again.

On the afternoon of the fourth day Adam sat up in bed. His head spun, but he could see the room well enough by light coming through a small window, its wooden shutter propped open with a stick. Marek was seated on a stool across the room, his long legs stretched out in front of him, his head leaning against the wall, eyes closed. Before that moment Adam had not clearly seen the man. He'd felt Marek's presence and been aware of his voice, but his mind had been too fogged and his vision too blurred to fully notice Marek's appearance.

Marek's tunic was unlaced at the neck so that the thick hair on his chest showed through; the tunic was belted low on his hips. He was neither young nor old, about the same age as Danusha, Adam guessed. His hands were broad and looked strong, his bare legs were hard-muscled.

"You said you knew my mother." Adam found it hard to speak clearly.

"You're awake! Really awake." Marek reached the bed in two strides. "You look better, Adam. How do you feel?"

"Not strong," he answered, "but my head doesn't hurt so much. I can think now. Where are we?"

"At an inn. Don't you remember coming? We left Krakow in the rain, but you were insensible most of the time we traveled. Do you remember any of it?"

"Bandages . . . you said I was your brother, burned in a fire."

"You do remember. You were so weak, I was afraid you had already been harmed by poison in the blood from your sores. But your face is beginning to heal now, and your eyes aren't so swollen."

"My mother," Adam said. "Tell me how you know her."

"Once many years ago," Marek answered, "before you were born, I was a guest in Pan Lucas's manor house. I met your mother then."

"Is that all? And because of that you went to so much trouble for me?"

Marek nodded. "Just because of that."

Adam lay back on the bed, not satisfied with the explanation, but still not thinking rationally enough to form any further questions. "I'm hungry," he said.

"Good. Glad to hear that. I'll go down and get some soup for you."

"I'm tired of soup," Adam said irritably. "I want something I can chew."

Marek laughed aloud. "You must be getting better, Adam. You're well enough to be tempersome."

The next day Adam was able to walk around the room. He asked Marek again about Danusha, but the man seemed to evade his questions, answering no more than he had the day before. He did explain to Adam, though, all the details of their escape—the forged document, the help he had received from Janus and Viktor. "It worked out even better than I'd hoped," he said. "I thought I'd have to leave the letter for Klemens, but after he looked at it, I took it with me. Now he'll have no way to trace my little handiwork. But as soon as you're well enough to sit a horse, Adam, we ought to leave this place."

"Are you going to take me home to my mother?" Adam asked.

"That would be too dangerous. Klemens has probably learned by now that you're not in a cell in Wawel Castle. The first place he'll look for you is Krol Forest. Since your mother doesn't know what has happened to you, she won't be able to give any information about your whereabouts, but I'll be less anxious after we get a good deal farther away from Krakow."

"Where will we go?"

"I want to travel north to the Poznan district where I live. I've arranged to buy a second horse from the innkeeper—it's a quiet mare, and I can lead her while you ride." Marek leaned over to put both hands on Adam's knees. "I've thought of a place where you'll be safe, but you must tell me if you are afraid to go there. The Franciscan brothers have a hospital not far from my manor. They care for people who are blind and sick. Some of the people have terrible, wretched diseases. Would you be fearful to stay there for a while?"

Adam hesitated, puzzled by Marek's question. He had been very ill himself—why should he be afraid of other sick people? He shook his head. "For a long time I wished I would die," he said, "while Klemens kept me in that cage. He said he was going to have me burned. Since God has seen fit to spare me, he must want me to stay alive for some reason. I won't be afraid to be around diseased people."

"Good. I'll take you there as soon as you can travel. Then I'll go home and send one of my men to Krakow to make certain that Janus and Viktor are in no trouble. After that . . ." He smiled at Adam. "I'll ride to Krol Forest to tell your mother that you're safe."

At last Adam realized the question he needed to ask Marek, one that had been skirting the edges of his consciousness since he'd awakened the day before. "When you saw me in the cage, how did you know that I was Danusha's son?"

"Oh." Flushing slightly, Marek got to his feet and went to prop the shutter open wider. He seemed to take longer than necessary to adjust the shutter, fiddling with the stick. Then, without looking at Adam, he said, "Janus told me. I'm going to go down now to see whether the horses are getting enough grain."

Marek strode swiftly across the room and fastened the door behind him.

Chapter 18 / *October 1399*

Adam pulled his stool as close as he could to the small brazier in his cubicle. He'd added a few sticks to the fire for light, although he welcomed the warmth, too. The room was always cold when the wind blew hard outside as it was doing that evening.

In late summer when Adam had first come to the Franciscan hospital, he'd enjoyed the coolness provided by the thick stone walls of the monastery adjacent to the hospital. But as autumn frosts whitened the roofs, he found that he was always chilly.

He examined the seal on the letter that had just been brought to him, finding no imprint on the wax. Breaking it open, he unfolded the paper and held it close to the fire to read it.

> *My dear son,*
> I will not put down names on this page. That way if it should fall into the wrong hands, none of our friends will be harmed. The person writing this letter for me is our oldest friend, who gave us shelter when we needed it most. He says that you will have no trouble reading what he writes, that he always knew you could read far better than your brother.
> A man whom I once knew as a squire came to tell me where you are, and that you are safe. My heart rejoiced at the news. He told me all that had happened. God will bless him for helping you.
> What you read next will surprise you, and I hope you will be

happy for me. I am going to be married. The captain who was kind to you has asked me to be his wife. Never did I think that I would be able to love a man again, but I do love him. He is good to your brother and me; he has arranged for your brother to study under a master sculptor. Please be glad for us.

May God be good to you, my son, and protect you from any further suffering. I will send messages to you whenever I can, and hope that when the weather grows warm again I can visit you.

Your Mother.

Adam read the letter again and again to understand the meaning of his mother's guarded words. Brother Vincenty had written the letter for her—that much was clear. And Pan Marek had gone to her with news of Adam. But she was going to marry Captain Pavel!

Adam was disturbed by the idea. Yet his mother was only thirty-three years old, young enough to have another husband, even more children. Adam pictured Danusha next to Pavel . . . in the man's arms. He rubbed his forehead with the heel of his hand as though to wipe away the image.

Since the day he'd overheard his mother talking with Brother Vincenty, Adam had blamed himself for her isolation. Now she was going to start a new life, just as Adam was doing. So why should the news of her marriage disturb him? Pavel was a good man, a decent man.

As Adam brooded in the dim firelight, turning the letter in his hands as though looking for more understanding than the words themselves could give him, he had to admit the truth. He did not want to be displaced as the most important person in his mother's life. Of course, Danusha loved Marcin; but Adam had known from his earliest years that the bond uniting his mother to her first son was stronger—in spite of the vexation and bitterness that sometimes flared between them—than Danusha had ever felt for Marcin.

He refolded the letter and put it inside his robe, the gray

robe of a novice in the Franciscan Order. He wondered how Marcin felt about their mother's marriage. Strange, he thought, Marcin has always wanted to be a woodcarver, and now, because of Pavel, he has the chance to become one. I've always wanted to be a monk, and God has led me to the Franciscans in this hospital. I asked the queen for a miracle, but perhaps God knew what he was doing all the while.

In the beginning Adam had been afraid to approach the abbot about whether he could be received into the Order, afraid he'd be rejected because of his ugliness. After the first few weeks, when he summoned enough courage to mention it, the abbot said, "We already feel that you belong with us, Adam. I have been much impressed by your attitude toward the sick. Perhaps it is because of the suffering you endured, but never have I seen so much compassion in one as young as you."

Vespers had rung some time ago; Adam had the better part of two hours remaining before he had to go to chapel for Compline. He decided to ask the abbot for paper and ink so that he could write to his mother. It might be a long while before the letter could be sent, depending on whether anyone traveling to Krol Forest should stop for lodging at the monastery, but he wanted to write Danusha that he approved of her marriage to Pavel. Though in truth the idea unsettled him, in conscience he knew that it was right for her. By the time the letter reached Danusha, Adam hoped he would have learned to accept her marriage with good grace.

He opened the door of his cubicle to find a monk standing outside it, his fist raised to knock. "I was sent by the abbot to summon you, Brother Adam," the monk said. "A visitor is waiting for you in the refectory. A nobleman, the abbot said."

"Thank you, Brother." Pleased, Adam hurried down the cold hall. Marek had promised to visit after he returned from

Krol Forest, and Adam was anxious to learn more about Danusha and Marcin and the wedding plans. It seemed uncanny that Marek should arrive on the very same day as Danusha's letter.

The door to the refectory was standing partway open; Adam was about to knock, but it seemed unnecessary. He went inside smiling, ready to greet Pan Marek.

But it wasn't Marek who waited for him.

The stranger stood at the far end of the room away from the firelight, his back toward the door. A white cape hung from his shoulders. The cape was marked with a black cross.

"Sir," Adam began hesitantly, "I am Brother Adam. I was told that someone was waiting here for me."

The man turned. He was so far in the shadows that Adam could not see his face. "Stand beside the fire, please," he said. "Let me look at you."

Adam did what the man asked, although he was becoming frightened. Marek had assured him that Warden Klemens could never find him at the hospital, but why else would a strange nobleman come looking for him?

"Do not be fearful," the man said. "I have come with only the best intentions. Are you the son of Danusha who once lived on Pan Lucas's estate?"

Adam nodded.

"Pan Marek told me about you. I have been away from Poland, or he would have told me sooner. I came as soon as I learned."

The man walked forward out of the shadows. In his gloved hands he held a steel helmet decorated with peacock feathers. His face was covered by a leather mask.

Adam was startled by the strange appearance of the man. Why would a nobleman keep his face covered in that manner? Then Adam's breath caught in his throat, and before he was aware of it he had spoken the name, "Reinmar!"

161

The man seemed taken aback. "Do you know me?"

"No! I . . ." Adam's mind raced in a confusion of remembered phrases. "Are you in truth Reinmar?"

"I am Count Reinmar von Galt of the Teutonic Order. And you are Adam von Galt, my son." He lifted his hand as though to touch Adam, then let it drop. "How did you know who I am?"

Adam hugged his chest with his arms to control his agitation. "I . . . didn't know . . . for certain. Once I overheard my mother talking to Brother Vincenty. She said my father's name was Reinmar. That . . . he always kept his face covered."

"I am he." Reinmar crossed the room to close the door tightly, then pulled off his gloves and let them fall to the floor. He raised his hands to remove the leather helmet. Adam stared enthralled, as the mask slipped away to reveal the man's face. It was covered on the cheeks and forehead by black hair streaked with gray. Scars pulled the skin— Reinmar's eyelids were misshapen just as Adam's were. Reinmar lifted his long mustache, saying. "My teeth, you see? Red like yours."

Adam could not stop staring at the face so much like his own, at the scarred hands. Though the man was taller and older, Adam had the unreal feeling that he was staring at his own image.

"Until Pan Marek came to me," Reinmar was saying, "I did not know that you had even been born. I was dismayed . . . no, I was filled with grief, Adam, to learn of your suffering. Now I've come to make it up to you."

Adam was too confounded to speak. "Let's sit down, shall we?" Reinmar suggested gently. "You look as though you need to sit. No more than I do, though." When he pulled forward a wooden armchair to rest beside one already in front of the fire, Adam sank into it, glad that he didn't have to depend on his unsteady legs to hold him upright.

162

"Marek tells me that your mother is planning to marry," Reinmar continued. "I'll settle a comfortable sum of money on her so that she never has need for anything. As for you, Adam, I intend to petition for your legitimacy so that you can inherit my estate in Germany."

Adam looked at the man in wonder, holding so tightly to the arms of the chair that his fingers cramped.

"You can live any way you want to," Reinmar told him. "But I hope you will choose to live with me." Reinmar shifted in the chair to look at Adam, obviously waiting for some response.

"How did Marek know?" Adam whispered.

"He was my squire for four years. When he saw you in Krakow, he recognized my affliction in you." Reinmar fingered his face. "I am not used to being without my mask, but you have a right to see me. You and I will become acquainted, Adam. We can begin when I take you to my family's estate in Germany."

Adam was shaken—the words struggled to form in his throat. "I can't go!"

"Because you've taken the vows of a novice?" Reinmar asked. "Those vows can be loosed. Only final vows are binding. I've served in my own order for long enough now; I'll resign my office so that you and I can live together, Adam. Since Queen Jadwiga's death, relations between Poland and the Teutonic Order have been badly strained. There will undoubtedly be war in the years to come, and I refuse to fight against Poland. After all . . ." This time when Reinmar reached out, his fingers pressed lightly against Adam's arm. "My only son is half-Polish."

Adam scrutinized the man's profile, so like his own, except that Reinmar was not nearly as scarred as Adam had become in Krakow. Though Adam's mind felt numbed, every detail of the man's face penetrated his vision with uncanny clarity: each hair, each scar, each distortion of the aristocratic fea-

163

tures. "Did you love my mother?" he blurted, half frightened by his own boldness.

"I did," Reinmar answered. His voice turned harsh. "I have never forgiven myself for the pain I caused her, and I have never stopped remembering her. If you could only have seen her, Adam, when I knew her . . . She was not only beautiful, she was so filled with life and strength! If God has ever forgiven me for what I did, it is because I was so . . . caught . . . by your mother's . . ." He stopped speaking to stare at the fire, his face rigid.

Adam could see that the man was distressed, but he didn't know how to comfort him. He was still stunned by this Reinmar whom he'd never expected to meet, still unable to comprehend that the man was his father.

"It's in the past, isn't it?" Reinmar asked, turning his head. "Now we must be concerned with the future. In little more than two months a whole new century will begin, and you and I will be together. What would you like to do? Shall we go to Germany first, so that I can show you the land you will inherit?"

"Sir," Adam said haltingly, "I have no use for land. When I take my final vows, one of them will be to live in poverty."

Reinmar frowned. "It is not necessary for you to become a monk. I've already told you . . ."

"I want to join the Franciscans," Adam broke in. "I'm happy here. I don't want to leave the hospital."

Reinmar stood up and walked to the fire, kicking a log so that the blaze flared to illuminate his disfigured face. "You had a very bad experience in Krakow, Adam," he said. "You must think the world is filled with treachery. But I'm a wealthy man, and wealth buys respect. I can protect you." He stood before Adam, seeming strong and assured, leaning forward persuasively. "I can take you to Italy, to see great cathedrals and statues carved by masters. Or we could live on my estate. I've never had much time for the leisurely pastimes

164

of noblemen, but we could hunt together, Adam, and I'll hire tutors if you want to be educated."

Adam felt as though he were drowning in Reinmar's words; he became even more unsure of himself. "I've always wished I could learn more. But you see . . . sir . . ." He didn't know how he should address Reinmar. "Here in the hospital, no one cares how I look, and I forget that I'm different. Some of the people who come here have such terrible diseases that they look worse than I do. And I like working with the sick. The abbot says I have compassion."

"Then it's evident what you must do." Reinmar spoke decisively. "You obviously have a quick mind. If you like working with sick people, you should be trained as a physician. I will arrange for it."

Adam hunched forward. So much had happened all at once to unsettle him; first the news that Danusha was going to marry Pavel, then the arrival of this imposing nobleman who was his father. He felt bewildered and off balance, too callow to know how to deal with the man who towered over him.

Through the confusion of his feelings rose a surge of anger. What right did this man have to appear out of nowhere, demanding to take control of Adam's life, the life which had so recently fallen into a satisfying path? He said he would protect Adam, but where had he been when Danusha and Adam needed protection—from the serfs who stoned them, from the loneliness of Krol Forest, from Klemens' torture? Resentful, he half rose in his chair to confront Reinmar. Then he looked into his father's eyes.

The eyes were pleading. The tall, forceful man who seemed so self-assured implored Adam, without words. Reinmar's scarred fingers trembled; when he saw Adam's gaze on them, he thrust his hands behind him.

"I can see that I've come upon you too quickly," Reinmar said as Adam sank back into the chair. "You see, I've known about you for several days now. All the time I traveled here

165

I've been planning for our life together. But I did not consider your feelings. I cannot expect you to . . . respond to me . . . so soon."

"It's just that I'd already decided to spend my life in this hospital," Adam told him quietly. Reinmar's disappointment was so visible in his face that Adam felt the first stirrings of sympathy for his father. And the man's words—they promised so much—could Adam allow himself to be tempted by them? It was difficult enough to realize that he had a father, a living man of flesh and blood, without having to puzzle over all that Reinmar was offering him.

"You could still do that," Reinmar said, his tone less certain. "If you will ask for a few years' absence from the Franciscans, you can study to be a physician. All the while you're at the university—any university you choose—I'll stay with you. I'll care for you. Then, when you receive a degree in medicine, you can come back here and take your final vows."

"I need time to think about this," Adam said. "I have to talk to the abbot. I don't know what to tell you." His mind was filling with images of himself as a student, as a doctor who would know how to heal people like the ones he now helped to tend.

"We have all the time in the world," Reinmar said, looking long into his son's eyes. "Now that we know each other."

Chapter 19

By early November the snow stood less than a foot deep in Krol Forest, but the weather was so cold that their breaths came in clouds of vapor. Adam noticed that his father's beard was thinly coated with rime.

"Not much farther now," Adam said to Reinmar. "You see, the trees are beginning to thin."

They had left their horses in the stables of the Cistercian monastery. Adam had said that the path was too narrow for two horses abreast, and in places would be difficult for a single horse and rider, but in truth he wanted to walk one more time through the forest that had been home to him for so much of his life.

When they reached the clearing where the cottage stood with smoke rising in gray curls from its stone chimney, Reinmar said, "You go in alone, Adam. I'll wait here for a time. They do not expect us, and it might be better if . . ."

Adam hesitated, knowing his father was right, yet not knowing what he was going to say to his mother about the astonishing turn his life had taken. How would she react? She had loved Reinmar, but now she was married to Pavel.

He stamped his feet as though he were intent on shaking the snow from his boots. Behind him, sensing his concern, Reinmar said, "It will be all right, Adam. Go in to your mother. I'll come when you call me."

Adam approached on the cleared path to the cottage. With

each step his concern was overridden by his eagerness to see his mother and Marcin, so that when he was almost there he broke into a run. Then he hurled himself against the door, flinging it open.

Marcin had been straddling the bench, carving. He threw down the knife and leaped to his feet, yelling, "It's Adam!" He bounded across the room, pulling Adam into Danusha's embrace. She clutched Adam so tightly that he almost lost his breath; all the while she wept and laughed and covered his cheeks with kisses as Pavel grasped his hand and then stepped back so that Marcin, too, could hug Adam.

"How did you come here?" Danusha cried. "We thought you were in Poznan! Is it safe for you . . ."

"Safe enough," Adam assured her, pulling back so that he could look at her. She wore no wimple; her braided hair was coiled around her head. Her face seemed thinner, and the lines at the corners of her mouth had deepened. "At least for a short time, Mother," he added. "Brother Vincenty told us that no one from Klemens has come to the monastery for more than two months."

"Told us? Told who? Is someone with you?"

"Yes. He's waiting outside."

"Pan Marek?"

"No. Someone else. You had better sit, Mother," Adam said. "I have a lot to tell you."

Danusha first grew pale, then flushed with color as Adam related how Reinmar had found him at the Franciscan monastery, how he'd waited for longer than a week until Adam decided, of his own choosing, to leave the Franciscans for the time it would take him to be trained as a physician. "We're going to the university in Padua—that's in Italy— where there's a famous school of medicine. Father said that both he and I will be safer in Italy than in Poland for the next few years, because King Jagiello is none too fond of the Teutonic Knights. But even if war breaks out before I finish

168

my studies, Father believes that he can return me safely to the Franciscan monastery. Before that, though, he wants to take me to Germany to meet his kin. *My* kin," Adam announced, feeling again the wonder that he had kin whom he'd never suspected existed.

"Adam," Pavel said, "your father is outside in the cold. Bring him in."

"I'll go with you to get him," Marcin said, taking Adam's arm as they went through the door. "Adam, remember that day," he whispered, "when you told me about Reinmar? You said we had two different fathers. In truth, we didn't have any father then, but now each of us has a father. You have Reinmar, and I have Pavel."

As the brothers led Reinmar into the cottage, they found Pavel waiting with his arm placed protectively around Danusha's shoulders. It was Pavel who took Reinmar's hand in greeting, Pavel who invited him to sit by the fire to thaw himself. Danusha stood silent while Reinmar answered Pavel in short phrases.

At last Reinmar broke the silence between the two of them. "Have I your permission to take Adam to Italy?" he asked Danusha.

"It seems that Adam has already made that decision," she answered.

"But I would prefer that you approved it."

Danusha cast down her eyes. "How long will he be away from Poland?"

"Three years, perhaps four. He can send you letters often. I'll see that they are delivered by paid messengers."

"Then the letters should be sent to Krakow," Pavel said. "The three of us will go to live there in the spring. I've been assigned to duty in the castle, and Marcin will study with the sculptor who is decorating Saint Mary's Church."

"So both of us will be learning what we want, Marcin," Adam broke in. "I wish you could go to Italy, too—Father

169

tells me that the handsomest sculptures are found there. I didn't tell you—as we travel I'll wear a leather headgear just like Father's."

Speaking rapidly because he wanted to share his excitement with the people he loved, Adam went on, "People may think it strange to see two men in such headgear, but Father is going to tell them that both of us have been afflicted with boils—like Job—because we drove a holy begging monk from our land. People will believe that, you know. Father will say that we've vowed not to remove our masks because of our shame, both over the boils and over our cruelty to the holy man. Wasn't it clever of Father to think of such an explanation?"

Danusha was staring at Adam, unsmiling, the color high on her cheekbones. She turned abruptly. "I'll set out bread and meat. You must want to eat after your travels."

"Set out nothing for me," Reinmar told her. "Brother Vincenty is waiting for me to eat with him. Adam can stay with you for as many days as you want, but I won't return here. When he's ready, Adam can join me at the Cistercian monastery."

As the woman of the house, Danusha should have attempted to persuade Reinmar to stay, at least for a glass of ale. Like every other Polish woman, she'd been taught from infancy that hospitality takes precedence over any ill feelings, that a guest in the house is like God in the house. Yet she said nothing, deliberately lowering her eyes as she stood with her knuckles pressed hard against the table.

Only Marcin was oblivious to the tautness in the room—he reached out to finger the embossed leather in Adam's new belt. After an awkward moment, Pavel said, "You must know that you're welcome here, Count Reinmar. I myself will bring Adam to the monastery in a few days; then I can make my farewells to you. Danusha"—he gestured to her, beckoning firmly—"walk our guest past the clearing. You surely want to thank him for all he's going to do for Adam."

Danusha opened the wooden chest and took out her gray cloak trimmed with squirrel fur. While Reinmar bade good-bye to Marcin, she waited beside the door, responding to Adam's beseeching look with a slight, stiff nod.

Outside, Danusha wrapped the cloak tightly around her against the cold of the late afternoon; though sunlight shone brightly on the fallen snow, the air was frosty. "It's still a warm cloak," she remarked, "after all these years. It has worn well."

"As you have, Danusha. Time has been gentle with you."

She turned her head, unwilling to acknowledge the compliment. "I notice that Adam has a new cloak," she said, "which you must have bought him."

"Yes," Reinmar replied, "made from the heavy wool sheared and woven in the High Tatra mountains."

She nodded, remembering.

"Your husband seems a good man," Reinmar said.

Danusha answered, "I've known none better. Or kinder."

Reinmar looked down, pushing snow into mounds with the toe of his boot. After a while he said, "You still haven't told me whether you are willing for Adam to go off with me."

"Does it matter whether I'm willing?" she asked, her voice rising. "Adam speaks of nothing but you. 'Father says, Father thinks . . .' It seems he won't miss me overmuch."

"God's breath, Danusha, what kind of talk is that! Of course he'll miss you. You shouldn't fault the lad because he takes pleasure in having a father at last." Reinmar kicked the mounds of snow, then turned so that he did not face her. "If only I had known, Danusha. I thought you would have settled on Pan Lucas's estate with a husband and children."

"Yet you never came to find out," she said.

He hunched his shoulders, disheartened. "You have every

right to feel harshly toward me," he said. "There's no way that I can make up to you for your years of trouble. But I swear to you—on every bit of honor that remains to me—that I will do all in my power for our son."

"Then I ask nothing more." He had to bend his head to hear her because she spoke so low. She was struggling with a truth that, if she were going to be honest, she had to admit to him. "The blame is not all yours, Reinmar. Twice I had the chance to send word to you about Adam, but I chose not to. Once when he was just a baby, and when I first came to Brother Vincenty for help."

From the cottage came the sound of laughter, Adam's and Marcin's, and Danusha knew that they were finding joy in their reunion. Pavel's deep voice joined theirs.

Letting the hood fall back from her face, she looked long at Reinmar, noticing how much he had changed. His beard was more gray than black, and his head seemed to sit lower on his shoulders, which had thickened and rounded with the passage of years. His dark eyes—once they had glittered with authority—now appeared anxious and shadowed. He no longer wore the distinguished white cape of the Teutonic Knights, but was wrapped in a plain cloak of the same grayish wool as Adam's, which he held tightly against him as though the cold were an enemy to be warded off.

He's growing old, she realized, and what has he had to warm his life? The resentment which had flared in her that afternoon succumbed to sympathy. Danusha reached to touch his leather mask with her fingertips, then raised her mouth and kissed him gently.

"I have happiness now," she told him. "Why should I deny you happiness? Take Adam, and go in peace."

The door burst open and Adam ran toward them, his face ruddy from the fire and full of good humor from the companionship he had just left. "Come, Mother," he said, throwing an arm around her—he was taller now by half a head. "Let's walk Father past the clearing."

"No," Danusha answered, "you walk with him. I've become chilled to the bone. I'll go back inside." She was not really cold; the cloak had always comforted her and always would.

Midway along the path, she turned to watch the two men depart from her.

Author's note

Reinmar and Adam suffered from erythropoietic porphyria, an inherited disease so rare that only seventy confirmed cases have been recorded in medical history. Victims of this incurable disease have an excess of porphyrins, red dyes, in the blood, which causes their bones, teeth, and urine to become red.

The most apparent symptom of the disease is extreme sensitivity of the skin to sunlight. As a protective mechanism, the body causes hair to grow on parts of the skin that are exposed to sun. Heavy scarring can tighten the skin around the sufferer's eyes, nose, mouth, and ears, creating an animal appearance.

Because these victims often avoided sunlight and came out only at night, and because they looked so frightening, it is not surprising that superstitious people believed them to be wolf-men.

About the Author

Gloria Skurzynski was born in Duquesne, Pennsylvania, and attended college in Pittsburgh. For as long as she can remember she has been interested in history, and she is an avid reader of historical fiction and non-fiction.

From one of her daughters, a doctor, she learned about the dread disease which causes its victims to become werewolf-like in appearance. This led to further investigation, and the writing of *Manwolf*.

Ms. Skurzynski has written eleven books for young readers, including, *What Happened in Hamelin,* a tale that combines legend and historical fact to tell the story of the fabled Pied Piper. It received a Christopher Award in 1980. *Manwolf* is her first book for Clarion.

The mother of five grown daughters, Ms. Skurzynski lives in Salt Lake City, Utah.

ABCDEFGHIJ—BP—876543210/81